MW01230807

ISBN: 978-1-61752-209-3

MURDER IN THE BACKWATER

A Lainey Maynard Mystery Series Book 2

LAURA HERN

CONTENTS

THANK YOU

Thank you for supporting authors by buying, reading, and reviewing our books. I give you my utmost gratitude! I couldn't continue to tell stories if it weren't for you and for the support team that surrounds me!

SOCIAL MEDIA

Laura Hern Social
Website & Newsletter:
https://www.laurahern.com

Facebook:
https://www.facebook.com/laurahernauthor

Also in series:
The Family Tree Murders
Curtain Call At Brooksey's Playhouse
Christmas Corpse At Caribou Cabin
And more coming soon!

REVIEWS AND PRAISE

This is a great series. It is light, full of interesting characters and a deep dark mystery! It made me laugh. It made me want to keep reading. It made me wonder. I can't wait for the next one. The Whoopee Club is quite the mystery solving team!
Karla

Once again Laura Hern has delivered a very fun read. She never disappoints.
Enjoy a quick, fun read.
Mary

It's a masterpiece! Fraud investigator Lainey Maynard is told to see one of their insurance customers. The man wants them to investigate the supposed murder of his wife. The mystery has many surprising twists and turns. Highly recommended!
Jerri

INTRODUCTION

Two Months ago

Lainey Maynard had been licking stamps for more than an hour. "My tongue is so dry, it's sticking to the roof of my mouth!"

Francy dropped the ink pen she was holding and rubbed the fingers on her right hand. "You think that's bad? My hand is cramped into a permanent claw from addressing these envelopes."

"You both volunteered to help me," Della reminded them. "I told you I had some mailings to do."

"Some mailings? This is the third batch! We must be close to a thousand," Francy said.

"Twelve hundred to be exact," Della grinned.

Lainey and Francy groaned at the same time.

"I'll make a pot of coffee," Vera said. "And I've got sugar cookies fresh from the oven."

Della smiled and looked at the stacks of letters in front of her. "Why does Mirror Falls have to mail out these notices for the Governor's office? He's the Governor, for Pete's sake. I'm sure he has a budget for postage!"

"It's not some fishing weekend," Francy replied. "It's the official start of the fishing season. It's a big deal to have it in Mirror Falls."

"Paul says it brings a ton of tourists to town... and they spend money," Della said.

Francy leaned back in her chair. "It's political. Don't let anyone tell you it is anything else."

Vera brought the coffee pot to the table and poured a cup for each of the girls. "It's been that way since I can remember."

"Fishing and politics," Lainey mused. "Seems like odd bedfellows."

"Every news station in the state will have reporters here. Sarge will put all his officers on duty for that night," Francy said. "Things can get out of hand quickly."

"I remember," Vera nodded. "Doc planned on being called to the emergency room at least three times that first night."

"People get hurt fishing?" Della asked.

"Sure they do. Dad took fish hooks out of cheeks, ears, and hands. Do you know where the most injuries occur?" Francy questioned.

"In the Governor's boat," Vera stated. "Those darn politicians have a quick temper!"

Lainey shrugged her shoulders. "Grown men fighting over the size of fish they caught?"

"Oh, they're catching a lot more than fish," Francy grimaced. "You'll see."

Vera glanced at Francy and then at Lainey. "Honey, you have no idea how much trouble hosting the fishing opener is going to be. Mirror Falls might never be the same."

Goosebumps suddenly covered Lainey's arms and she felt a little nauseous.

Something's going to happen. I can feel it. Do I dare tell them?

CHAPTER 1

For six months of the year, Mirror Falls transforms from a popular tourist vacation destination for boaters, campers, bikers, hikers, and baseball fans, into a deserted ghost town.

Old Man Winter's frigid winds, below zero temperatures, and mountains of snow force each resident into hibernation. The days when the grey sky gods allowed the sun to briefly peek its head out from among the dreary clouds could be counted on one hand. The past winter had been unusually long and bitter with more than 90 inches of the white stuff falling from October through late March.

Cabin Fever, as the locals called it, gripped every member of every household. Dogs, cats, and hamsters in town had it, too. The fever showed no mercy. Even houses felt its wrath.

Utility rooms and mud rooms were cluttered with piles of heavy down-filled coats, plaid woolen scarfs, hats and gloves, and well-worn snow boots covered with salt stains from the months of residue left on the roads. Scarred snow shovels and tired snowblowers stood in reverent silence by the garage doors, ready for action again on a moment's notice.

By the time April arrived, Cabin Fever had transformed the kindest, most even tempered of the locals into angry, impatient, caged animals chomping at the bit to escape the confines of their homes. Conversation at the local coffee shops revolved around one topic... the Minnesota Governor's Fishing Opener. It was the annual affair that kept hopes alive and locals from killing each other during the long winter.

"It's Cabin Fever, I tell you," Shep Morton said as he handed Vera the takeout food she'd ordered. "I'm getting sick and tired of cranky customers."

Vera frowned at his remark and nodded. "Oh, I know all about that. Doc referred to it as GBS... Grumpy Blues Syndrome."

"I bet he saw a bunch of angry and depressed patients. They're all crazy."

"A few of them thought he was Dear Abby! He'd have perfectly healthy patients come in and expect him to sit and listen to their complaints."

"Gossip central, that's what Doc's office was. Bet he had stories to tell you."

She picked up her box and turned to leave. Stopping short of the restaurant door, she turned and looked back.

"Are *you* still feuding with Charlie at the Bait Shop?"

He squinted his eyes in her direction.

"The supply committee voted to buy all the bait from him this year."

Shep set his jaw and stared out the window.

"The last food committee meeting is tonight. See you there," she grinned, opened the door, and made sure it slammed shut behind her.

"Darned old goat!" she said aloud as she got into her car. "How Sally ever put up with him is beyond me."

The Whoopee group decided to meet this week at Francy's house instead of going out to one of the regular eating spots. With only a week left before the fishing opener, each was on at least one committee and needed to spend time working on various tasks. Vera had volunteered to pick up something for dinner and the ladies were sitting at the dining room table waiting for her.

Francy looked down at her watch. "Mom said she'd be here no later than 5:30. It's already 6:15. I apologize that she's late, again."

"Wasn't she going to pick up supper from the Backwater?" Lainey asked.

"Yes, and I'll bet she and Shep are wasting time arguing about something or other."

Lainey and Della looked at each other and grinned.

"What's the story, Francy?" Della asked. "Spill the beans."

"It's a ridiculous ongoing feud that started when Shep and Charlie bowled on the same team."

"Bowling?" Lainey couldn't help smiling. "In a bowling league?"

Della rested her elbows on the table. "Paul said bowling was a *big deal* back in the day."

"It was. During the winter, bowling alleys were the only places open. All of the towns around Mirror Falls had leagues and hosted tournaments," Francy stated. "Women's leagues, men's leagues, mixed leagues… anything that could stand on two legs and manage to throw a bowling ball down the alley joined a league."

Lainey shook her head in amazement. "I've never heard of a bowling feud lasting fifty years. What did they argue over?"

Francy looked at the wrinkled tablecloth and grinned.

"Does Vera know, Francy?" Della asked.

"Dad might have told her."

Lainey caught the sly look between the two.

"All right. Tell me what happened," she demanded.

The doorbell rang and Francy got up to answer it. Vera came inside, apologizing for being late.

"Hi, girls," she stated, handing the food to Francy then taking off her shoes and coat. "I've got comfort food… meatloaf, mashed potatoes, and gravy!"

The conversation during dinner was light and revolved around the upcoming event.

"It's your first time serving on the host board, Lainey. Is it awkward having Raymond as the chairman?" Della asked.

"You don't have to answer that, sweetie," Vera quickly chimed in. "We know it's hard for you."

Lainey twisted a piece of the tablecloth in her hands. She could feel her face flush and her entire body felt like she was in a sauna. Raymond Sullivan, the handsome CEO of the Sullivan's Best Poultry empire, had unexpectedly swept her off her feet. She hadn't dared become involved with anyone since she lost her husband. They had dated for a few months and she was happy. Until the day he called to inform her it was over.

His voice had been cold and distant. His words sharp and business like. "Lainey, you're a beautiful woman and I enjoy spending time with you. But I'm not ready for a serious relationship…"

She shivered at the memory of his voice, then tried to regain her composure.

"I don't have much contact with him," she shrugged her shoulders. "He doesn't attend many of the meetings."

"In my day, men were polite and respectful. If they needed to talk with you, they came to your house - face to face." Vera stated. "None of this face calling or face texting or whatever it is now."

Chuckling, Francy replied, "Mom, cell phones hadn't been invented when you were dating. Guys had to find a pay phone to call you back then. And it's FaceTime, not face calling."

"We had a home phone. Besides, who had a quarter for a pay phone?" Vera asked. "Are you okay, Lainey? I'm sure he hurt your feelings."

"I'm fine working on the committee. Raymond Sullivan is past history."

How I wish I were over him!

A quiet minute passed before Della broke the silence.

"The registration committee let me be the lead contact."

"You mean you got the short end of the straw when it came time to pick a chairman," Francy laughed out loud.

"Anyway," Della continued, trying hard not to smile, "I think we have five hundred entries so far. We've planned for at least twelve hundred."

"I've been studying up for the trivia contest again," Vera added. "I'm going to win that Mexico vacation package this year."

"What about Faye?" Della kidded. "Hasn't she beaten you the last several years?"

"She broke her hip in February and moved to Florida to live with her kids," Francy grimaced. "Of course you'll beat her, Mom."

"Well, you never know. She could send in an absentee ballot!"

The laughter that followed lightened the mood and Lainey was thankful for that. She didn't want to think about Raymond.

"I do have a dilemma," Della said. "Paul tells me that the opener is politically motivated. I'm having a difficult time trying to organize who is sitting in the boat with the Governor. Any ideas?"

Francy sighed. "Politically motivated is an understatement. It's all about politics… and money."

"How so?" Lainey piped in. "Money for the city, I can see. But what makes it benefit the Governor?"

"There are only two reasons to have an official fishing opener," Vera began. "The first is for local politicians to bend the Governor's ear and get special funds for their own interests. The second is a campaign photo opportunity for his re-election bid."

"Yep. All the major news stations will follow him like a hawk," Francy agreed. "It's ridiculous the amount of dollars spent protecting the Governor so news anchors can take his picture in front of a bar holding a Minnesota craft beer."

"Channel Ten kept showing a video of him sitting behind the wheel of a big ol' green John Deere tractor last year. The wind kept blowing his straw hat off!" Della laughed loudly. "He'd pick it up, try to pose, then it would fly off again."

Lainey rubbed her eyebrow and wrinkled her nose. "I thought it was to start the official fishing season in Minnesota."

"Oh, it is. But remember, we have more than 1.4 million licensed anglers in our state. Out of that, more than five hundred thousand will fish on opening day. And we have eighteen thousand miles of fishing streams and waters," Vera commented.

"You sound like a World Book Encyclopedia," Francy added, rolling her eyes.

"It's all in the trivia study guide. I told you, I'm going to win this year!"

"Back to my question, please," Della directed. "Whom should I put in the boat with the Governor? Can I put Democrats and Republicans in the same boat?"

Francy cleared her throat and sat up straight in her chair. "No! Only his party members in his boat. The opposing party is in the boat just behind him."

"Paul cautioned me to do that as well," Della answered.

Lainey thought she was joking. "Seriously? It's that important to keep them separate? It's just fishing, for Pete's sake."

Francy closed her eyes and nodded. "Fishing has nothing to do with."

"Years ago, Doc was in charge of the Governor's boat. Months prior to the opener, people took him out to lunch, bought him gifts, gave him tickets to sports games. They tried to bribe him to put them in the boat."

"How did he decide who got in?" Della asked.

"He put all the names in a bag, shook them up, and drew out six names."

"Well, I guess that's fair. Maybe I'll try that."

"Tell her the rest of the story, Mom."

Vera took a deep breath, then rolled her eyes. "The six whose names were drawn were happy. But twelve of those whose names weren't drawn, were terribly angry. They demanded to know how he made the decision and accused him of showing partiality. When he told them he drew names out of a bag, they accused him of cheating. They demanded he hold a public drawing with the news channels present."

Della shook her head in disbelief. "That's unbelievable. What did Doc do?"

"He told them to go jump in the lake, waders and all," Vera grinned.

Lainey chuckled.

"I think he later regretted his choice of words. Those twelve started a smear campaign. They spread rumors that his college internship had been falsified, that he was a drunk that was routinely seen in bars in St. Cloud, and that he had been sued for malpractice. It not only damaged his reputation, but his business suffered."

"All because Dad refused to redraw a few silly names," Francy shook her head and sighed. "It's entirely about politics."

Della's face went white. "Oh, dear. Now I know *why* they asked me to be the chairperson. I hope this doesn't do damage to Paul's reputation! What can I do?"

The group sat in silence, each one deep in thought.

"Why not let the Governor choose who he wants in the boat?" Lainey asked.

Francy rolled her eyes. "Absolutely not. He'd pick his cronies, for sure. The press would have a field day with that."

"I can see the headlines now," Vera winced. "Local Croaker's Wife Fills Governor's Boat With Hand-Picked Stink Bait."

Della shivered. "Good grief."

"Every entrant is assigned a number, correct? Well, since the purpose is to get free publicity for the Governor, why not hold a press conference and draw numbers, like a lottery," Lainey suggested.

"Hmm…" Francy said aloud. "That might work. People love lotteries. What do you think, Della?"

"If it means keeping Paul out of the line of fire, I'm all for it. I'll let the committee know tomorrow morning."

Vera sighed, clearly debating what she was about to say. "Why not hold the event at Backwater?"

The surprised look on Francy's face was unmistakable.

"Mom, why are you promoting Shep's place?"

"The committee is buying all the bait from Charlie this year."

"You told Shep, didn't you?" Francy said angrily. "You

know that just stirs up more trouble between him and Charlie."

Vera rolled her eyes and frowned. "Yes, I told him. So have your little ticket drawing at his place. That'll even things up."

"Vera!" Della groaned. "I'll try to persuade the committee."

As hard as she tried, Lainey couldn't stop grinning or chuckling.

"Don't you laugh," Vera said. "Shep's just a crusty old…"

"Della, I think Mom and Lainey need to be on hand for the drawing, don't you?" Francy winked.

"Oh, you better believe it. I'm not walking the plank alone!"

"Hmpf!" Vera grunted, crossing her arms.

CHAPTER 2

Della and Lainey spent much of the next two days organizing the press conference. What started as a small ceremony to draw names quickly snowballed into a full blown publicity event with hundreds of attendees. Suddenly, the two ladies found themselves taking orders, not giving them.

The Governor's office issued official invites. Mirror Falls dignitaries wanted to be front and center. Each of the major news stations would send crews with vans, cameras, and tons of reporters. Local law enforcement planned to beef up all security measures at the city's expense.

Della was constantly on the phone, listening to complaints or demands from the Governor's office, Sarge at the police station, and others.

Right in the middle of all the hustle and bustle was the Backwater restaurant. Shep was up in arms because the Governor's office sent a staging crew to *spruce up* the place before his arrival.

"My restaurant's been the same for forty years," Shep

growled into the phone. "I don't need some politician bringing in fancy new tables and chairs."

"My hands are tied," Della tried to console him. "It's out of my control."

"They're painting the walls Chartreuse green! What kind of color is *Chartreuse green?* Looks like a darn truck stop bathroom in here!"

"Remember, all those people need to eat somewhere. It'll be a big boost to your sales."

"They'd better stay out of my kitchen! That's all I'm saying."

Della sighed as she hung up the phone. *Why did I agree to this?* she thought to herself. She was running late for a meeting with Ben Sargent and hurried to put on her coat. Before she could get into her car and pull out of her driveway, she had missed three more calls. She let them all go to voice mail.

Sarge wanted to meet at Babe's House of Caffeine to clarify his officers' roles at the press conference. As she drove to the coffee house, her Bluetooth rang. Lainey's name appeared.

"Hello?" she said hastily as she answered the call.

"Rough morning, huh?" Lainey asked.

"It's a nightmare. It seems I'm the official complaint department!"

"Same here. I'm sorry I mentioned this press conference idea. Rose from the Governor's publicity committee called me. They told me Raymond Sullivan would be the person drawing the names."

Della didn't respond.

"He is chairman of the steering committee."

Still no response.

"It'll take the pressure off you and Paul. People will be angry with Raymond if their name isn't drawn."

"The Governor's office has taken over everything," Della said slowly.

Lainey hesitated, trying to think of the best way to phrase her reply.

"He's also going to be the Master of Ceremonies."

"They've asked him to welcome people and introduce the Governor?"

"I'm sorry, I know Paul had planned to do that."

"I see." Her voice, eerily monotone, didn't hide her disappointment.

"Francy and I are heading over to Babe's. We thought you might like a couple extra sets of ears when you meet with Sarge."

"Thanks. Maybe you can take notes for me?"

"Sure thing. We'll see you shortly."

Della disconnected the Bluetooth. She pulled into a parking space on the street in front of Babe's and turned off the car. She sat for a minute trying to gather her thoughts. She looked in the rearview mirror and wiped away the tears that had fallen. She got out of her car and headed toward the entrance.

"I've fought tougher bullies than this. They'll not get the best of this gal," she said aloud.

Sarge and Francy were waiting at a table and waved to her as she came in. She walked over, took off her coat and settled into the chair across from Sarge.

"I'm a little bit late," Della said. "I've been putting out fires." She grinned and then winked. "I'm wearing my boxing gloves…" she paused, "bring it on."

Lainey walked in the door and over to the table just in time to hear the words *bring it on*. She saw the startled look on Sarge's face and Francy was grinning from ear to ear.

"What did I miss?" she asked as she sat down.

"What's happened? Clue me in here." Sarge looked sternly at Della and then at Francy.

"Nothing at all, Sarge," Francy replied. "Regular fishing opener challenges."

Sarge shook his head and sighed. "Let's go over the logistics, Della, once more before heading over to the Backwater to start setting up. Here's a brief outline showing where our security will be, where we will setup a mobile headquarters, and the diagram for parking area barriers to be placed this afternoon."

"Why do I need this?" Della asked with a nonchalant tone in her voice. "I'm not in charge."

Sarge sat back in his chair. "We had agreed earlier that each one of you has an area to cover. Della is to make sure dignitaries are seated where they are supposed to be. Francy and one of my officers will be at the front entrance, checking credentials. Lainey is to monitor the media seating area and check press badges."

The three ladies nodded but said nothing.

Sarge stared at Francy and Lainey for a long moment, then focused his eyes on Della. "You've heard about Sullivan."

"Put your mind at ease, Sarge," she replied casually. "He's more than welcome to be the ringmaster for this circus." She motioned for the waitress. "Let's order lunch. I'm craving a double cheeseburger with tons of onions rings!"

Sarge shook his head and laughed. "Lunch is on me this time."

The four spent more than an hour eating lunch and planning for the next day's events.

"Time is getting away from us. I'm heading back to the station. Let's plan on meeting at Backwater in an hour. That will give my officers time to prepare."

The ladies thanked Sarge and walked out together.

"I'm proud of you, Della," Lainey said. "You handled yourself well."

"You know me. When I get pushed too far, I write the situation off. As far as I'm concerned, I'll do my assigned job, and nothing more."

"I can count on one hand the times Sarge has offered to buy lunch," Francy chuckled. "Guess it was his way of extending an olive branch."

"We've got an hour," Lainey said. "I think I'll head on over to the restaurant. I'm not too familiar with the inside and I'd like to look around before Sarge and his men arrive."

"Snoop around, you mean," Della kidded.

"That too! Where are you two headed?"

"I'm going to the funeral home first to fill in Paul. I'll meet you there."

Lainey nodded. "What about you, Francy? Wanna go with me?"

"You bet. I may need to run interference for you." Francy took a breath mint out of her coat pocket and popped it in her mouth.

"What's the breath mint for?" Della asked.

"Mom says Shep eats breath mints like they are going out of style. Thought I'd offer him one or two when I see him."

Lainey grinned. "Ah! Buttering him up. I like the sound of that! See you there."

The ladies hugged each other, then got in their cars.

The Backwater restaurant was a twenty-minute drive down Hwy 71 from Mirror Falls. The road wasn't normally patrolled by State Troopers, but visitors and news media caravans had flooded the area causing traffic to be heavier than usual. Troopers were positioned on both sides of the road and had cars pulled over in several spots.

Francy pulled up to the Backwater just a few seconds

before Lainey. The two got out of their cars and stopped in front of the path leading to the entrance.

Lainey glanced around the area and noticed that there was only one other building nearby. She looked at Francy.

"Why in the world did they decide to have the opener at this little spot? There's hardly enough room for our two cars to park."

"What better way for the Governor to gain favor with voters than to highlight their favorite local fishing hole. And you can be sure, he'll meet with a lot of residents and the television cameras will be rolling."

"I see. Who wouldn't want to be on the national news with the Governor?"

"Exactly. Let's go inside and find Shep."

The steppingstone path that led from the dirt parking lot to the entrance hadn't aged well. Some of the stones' corners had sunken and the winter melt had turned the grass growing between them into muddy patches, making it difficult to walk on the uneven path.

The building was a small two story house that sat thirty feet or so from the shoreline. The yellow paint had dulled over the years and a southern porch surrounded the entire place. It had once been painted white with ship plank as the railing and lattice work for decoration. A faded blue striped awning provided shade between the first and second floors. High top round tables and chairs allowed for more seating and in the summer months, a great view of the lake.

Inside, the two friends found an entourage of painters, scaffolding, and tools. The floor was completely covered in plastic and crackled when they walked on it. Somewhere a radio was blasting rock music and no one noticed they had walked inside.

"Shep?" Francy shouted as she made her way to the back of the restaurant. "Hey, Shep. It's Francy. Where are you?"

Lainey heard a loud bang and thought someone had slammed a heavy door. She saw a man wearing a white stocking cap and a stained apron making his way toward them.

"It's like a dang obstacle course in here. It's worse than KP duty in the Marines!" Shep grumbled. "Let's go out on the porch so I can hear you better."

He walked over to a set of sliding glass doors in the middle of one outside wall. He opened them, stepped onto the porch, and motioned for them to follow. He closed the door once they were outside.

"Did you bring Vera with you?"

"No, she couldn't come this time. But I know she'll be here tomorrow." Francy said smiling broadly. "This is Lainey Maynard, a friend of ours."

Lainey stepped forward and put out her hand.

"It's nice to meet you. Vera speaks highly of you." She shot a quick glance at Francy who was doing her best not to laugh.

"A Whoopee group member, I suppose. I recall reading about you in the paper," he said as he shook her hand.

Oh, great. Good old Mirror Falls gossip tabloid.

"Looks like the Backwater is getting a facelift," she commented, trying to change the subject.

His face wrinkled up causing his bushy eyebrows to almost touch each other.

"Sally and I painted this years ago. Did we paint it green? No. Do I want it painted green now? No!" He took a deep breath, then let it out slowly. "All this bunk because the *Governor* wants to *fish* here."

Lainey didn't say a word. She looked at Francy for help.

"Well, you know those darn politicians can be pushy," Francy replied. "It's a bother for sure. Maybe you'd be happier if they were painting next door at Charlie's Bait

Shop instead. How about a mint?" She reached into her pocket, pulled out the container, and held it close to him.

Shep grimaced and his jaw ground back and forth on his teeth. He took the container, shook out a large handful, and shoved it back at Francy.

He popped a few mints in his mouth. "Why are you two here? The police tribe isn't supposed to show up until 4 p.m."

"We're working tomorrow and wanted to be more familiar with the building. Mind if we look around before the crowd arrives?" Lainey asked.

Shep studied their faces before he spoke. "Go ahead. I've got nothing to hide."

Nothing to hide, eh? We'll see about that.

"Thanks. We won't get in your way," Francy replied.

"Everyone is in my way. You're on your own." He popped a few more mints into his mouth, opened the sliding door, and left them standing on the porch.

Francy smiled and looked at Lainey. "That was interesting."

"He's hiding or guarding something. We don't have much time before Sarge arrives. I'll take the kitchen and back area."

"I think I'll walk over to Charlie's. It gives me an excuse to look around the outside."

Lainey opened the door and walked toward the kitchen. The painters were cleaning up and didn't notice her. She found the door to the kitchen and went inside. It wasn't a big space and she was surprised how clean it looked considering the work being done in the front. She looked around for Shep but saw no one.

She walked through the cooking area, opening cabinets and closets, and found nothing but supplies and utensils. There were two tall freezers on one wall that had locks on their door handles. She noticed a hallway just to the left of them. She looked back to make sure no one was in the room and then walked down the hallway. There was a bathroom on one side and a maintenance room on the other. At the end of the hallway was a door with the words *Shep and Sally* stenciled on it in black paint.

Lainey put her ear to the door to see if she could hear anyone inside. When she heard nothing, she tried opening it. It was locked. She reached into her fanny pack, took out her credit card, and started to work on opening the lock.

"Glad I had to watch those videos using credits cards to open locks. Let's hope this works," she said aloud.

After a couple of tries, the door unlocked. She looked behind her quickly, then opened the door and went inside. She found the light switch, flipped it on, and closed the door. She expected it to be an office or something similar. Instead, she saw a small kitchen complete with a standing oven, double sink, a refrigerator, and some sort of island or chopping station. And hanging from a wooden rack beside the fridge were strands of dried-up fish entrails. Some of the skeletons still had skin on them.

Why would he have a kitchen inside his regular kitchen?

Her cell phone pinged signaling a text had come in. She quickly took her phone out of her fanny pack and read the text from Francy.

"Sarge is pulling in the parking lot."

Lainey quickly snapped a picture of the room with her phone. She opened the door and turned off the light. She reset the lock and shut the door, testing it to make sure it was locked.

She hurried back through the kitchen and into the dining room just as Sarge and his men were walking in. She was walking toward them when a man's voice from behind startled her. She stopped and turned around to see Shep glaring at her.

"Find what you were looking for?"

"Yes, you have a beautiful kitchen area. I'm looking forward to tasting your cooking tomorrow."

"I didn't hire you to cook. It gets really hot in my kitchen. Stay out or you might get burned."

She nodded and turned back around.

You might be surprised just how hot it can get.

CHAPTER 3

L ainey saw Della and Francy standing by the entrance, listening to Sarge giving orders. She walked over to stand by them and waited for the sergeant to finish. None of the three could have imagined the chaos that was soon to follow.

Sarge raised his hand as he finished speaking. "That's it for now. We've moved in a large fish house on the north side of the parking lot next to the bait shop. From this point going forward, that will be our base and main rendezvous point. Keep your radios open. Meet at the base at 20:00 hrs., sharp."

All at once, everyone was on the move. The officers talking on their radios, split off in different directions while the painting crew scampered to get out of their way. Media trucks trying to find a parking spot honked their horns. People were rushing around everywhere. The three ladies stood still in their small little corner, stunned and afraid to move.

Lainey shrugged her shoulders and raised her hands in surprise.

"Oh, my gosh! It's like watching a bunch of angry ants in a glass farm that someone shook up."

Francy nodded. "Welcome to a Sarge operation. It's organized chaos. But he gets the work done."

Della walked over to the front door and peered out. "Who let the media trucks in? The parking barriers haven't been setup yet."

"Maybe the best thing for us to do is…" Lainey was interrupted by Sarge's voice on a radio.

"Della, bring your diagram to the parking lot."

Francy looked at Della. "He gave you a radio? I thought you weren't going to be involved."

"Unfortunately, as chairman, I have a responsibility to help him. Paul was going to fill in for me, but he had an emergency at the funeral home."

"Want us to come with you?" Lainey asked.

"Sure. He'll have something for you to do."

They followed her out the door and down the stone path to the parking lot where Sarge had been surrounded by media people. They were all talking at the same time.

He held up his hand to quiet the crowd.

"Folks, you'll have to back your vehicles out the way you came. We're setting up several parking areas on the road leading to the restaurant. You were given a map of those areas when you registered. Please move your vehicles immediately or they will be towed."

There was a general moaning sound that arose from the crowd when he finished. Grumbling, they slowly returned to their vehicles and obeyed Sarge's orders.

Sarge shook his head and turned to face the ladies.

"Della, we're putting up a barricade across the parking lot entrance. In case a vehicle does drive up, I need a person stationed here to turn them around. You have a map and can show them where the designated parking areas are. Will you do that? I'll have an officer relieve you as soon as possible."

"Okay. What about Francy and Lainey? Want them to stand here as well?"

"That's fine. Francy knows the ropes and can handle any obstinate..." the sound of his radio interrupted him. "I'll be around if you have trouble." He answered the radio and walked away quickly.

"I never thought this little drawing event for a seat in a boat would turn into such a major headache!" Lainey remarked. "It's Mirror Falls, not New York City."

"This is nothing. Wait till tomorrow at midnight when the actual tournament begins," Francy said. "There'll be more boats trying to get on the lake than confetti dropped in Times Square on New Year's Eve."

The next few hours were not spent turning away media trucks or vans but dealing with a constant stream of anglers trying to get a jump on their competition by parking their boats behind the restaurant.

The most heated exchange occurred when Quincy Yelnick, owner of a small convenience store chain in the area, tried to enter.

"I'm sorry sir, but you'll have to turn around. Boat parking isn't open until tomorrow afternoon," Della said politely.

"Shep always lets me unload early. I donate food to his establishment."

"That's not the case this year. A map with instructions was included in your registration packet. You'll have to come back tomorrow."

"My name is Quincy Yelnick. Call Shep down here. He'll set you straight."

Francy walked over and stood beside Della. "Hello, Mr. Yelnick. Good to see you. In fairness to other contestants, we have to follow the rules. I think there's enough space for you to safely turn around."

Quincy's voice grew louder. "You don't work at the station anymore. I'm not going to fish, just going to park my boat."

"Sir, no one is allowed to park early. Please turn around and come back tomorrow."

Quincy put the car in park and turned off the engine. He opened the door and angrily stood between Della and Francy. He hadn't noticed that Lainey, who had been standing on the opposite side of his car, had gone to get help.

"Look, I'm going to park tonight. Get out of the way or get run over."

Della reached for her radio, but Quincy stopped her hand before she could use it.

"Think that radio will stop me?" He looked at Francy. "Think you can take me down?"

"No. But I will. Back off now and return to your vehicle." Sarge yelled as he hurried toward them. Even out of breath, his voice was commanding.

Quincy let go of Della's hand and turned to face Sarge.

"Back off, Yelnick. Get into your vehicle and leave. We're not looking for trouble tonight."

"I'm going to park the boat, then I'll leave."

"I'm warning you. Get in your vehicle and leave. No one is parking anything tonight."

The two glared at each other. Francy knew Sarge was prepared to pull his weapon if necessary. Moving slowly, she grabbed Della's elbow and began backing away from the angry men.

Seconds seemed like hours as the tension mounted between the two. Finally, Sarge broke the silence.

"This is your last warning. Get in your vehicle and leave."

Quincy rolled his neck around slightly as if to loosen it up.

"You tell Morton his supply of free meat just dried up."

Sarge watched closely as he opened the car door and got inside. He started the car, then paused to stare directly at the officer. He gunned the motor several times without breaking his gaze. Sarge didn't move a muscle.

Finally, he put the car in reverse and hastily turned around. He sped back down the road he had entered.

"Are you two okay?" Sarge asked walking toward Della and Francy.

Della lunged forward and gave him a big hug. "I'm so glad to see you!"

"Thanks, Sarge. I don't know how Lainey found you so quickly," Francy said.

"She called me and luckily I was close by."

"She called you? How?"

"I have his cell phone number on speed dial," Lainey laughed. She had been standing behind a tree as instructed by Sarge, and once the man drove off, she walked over to them. "I called as soon as the man started arguing with you."

"How did you know he wouldn't turn around?" Della asked.

"He had two rifles laying in his back seat. I could see them from where I was standing, but I knew you couldn't."

Della's face turned white. "As you are my witnesses, I will *never, ever* volunteer for anything again!"

"Yelnick is a troublemaker. People like him are few and far between. Why don't you three call it a night? My guys can take it from here. I'll see you tomorrow." Sarge smiled. He looked at Lainey and winked.

"Good thing I hadn't blocked your number, huh?" He grinned and walked away.

"Hey! I keep your life exciting," Lainey shouted after him.

"I'm exhausted and all the big worry stuff doesn't happen until tomorrow." Della moaned. "I'm going home, make myself a little hot toddy, and try to get some sleep."

"Sounds like a plan," Francy replied. "What time do you want us here to help you?"

"I plan on coming around 10 a.m. You know I'm not much of a morning person."

"We'll be here. Get some rest. It's all going to work out," Francy said trying to sound reassuring.

As Lainey drove home, her thoughts weren't on the hectic day that would follow. The strong feeling of dread that began in the pit of her stomach earlier that evening, now included a feeling of heaviness in her chest, too. She'd felt this same uneasiness twice before. And each time, something terrible had occurred.

She pulled into her garage, turned off the car, and waited for the garage door to close before getting out. She walked into the utility room, then, as an afterthought, turned around and walked back to the car. She locked the doors and returned to the house. Her cat was waiting for her.

"Hey, Powie," she said taking off her coat and putting her things on the counter. "Let's go sit in the recliner. Think I want to watch television for a while." She picked up the cat and walked into the living room. The next couple of hours were spent flipping through channels, trying to find something that would keep her interest. But her mind was whirling and spinning. Scenarios of all kinds of disasters that might happen at tomorrow's event kept flooding her thoughts.

Finally, she turned off the television, checked her cell phone one last time, and leaned back as far as she could in the chair. Powie was sleeping without a care in the world.

"Wish I could sleep as soundly as you do," she said to the cat.

She yawned and closed her eyes.

The loud ringing of her cell phone startled her awake. She sat the recliner up quickly, throwing the cat off her lap. She blinked several times and then answered the phone.

"Hello?"

"It's Francy. I just heard on the police scanner something has happened at the Backwater."

"Oh, no," she sighed heavily. See looked at the clock. 6:40 a.m.

"I'll pick you up in ten minutes, okay?"

"What about Della? Does she know?"

"I don't know."

"I'll be ready."

Lainey hung up and moved quickly. She changed into a clean sweatshirt, grabbed her backpack, and was waiting in front of the house when Francy pulled up.

"What's happened?" she asked as she got in the car.

"The call came in as officer needing assistance and a 10-37."

"Francy, speak in layman's terms. What's a 10-37?"

"Oh, sorry, I'm in police mode. It means there's a suspicious vehicle being investigated."

"Why is that a big emergency?"

"It depends on..."

The ringing of her cell phone interrupted her. She touched the car's Bluetooth to answer.

"Thought you'd want to know," the male voice said. "Sarge called in 10-52 and 10-79."

"Thanks." Francy ended the call.

"What? Who was that?"

"My friend at dispatch. Sarge requested an ambulance... and the coroner."

Lainey closed her eyes and shook her head.

Oh, no! I knew it. I knew something bad was going to happen. I felt it.

She was instantly nauseous and swallowed hard to keep from throwing up in the car. She couldn't say anything. She leaned forward in her seat, holding her head in her hands.

"You okay? Do I need to pull over?"

"I'll be okay. Let's just get to the Backwater."

CHAPTER 4

Two miles from the Backwater, Francy drove past cones and barriers of all sorts. Signs pointing the way to designated parking areas stood like little guard soldiers every fifteen feet or so.

"Someone worked all night to get this ready," Francy remarked.

The nausea had settled down and Lainey was sitting up, looking out her door window.

"When do the flaggers and parking attendants arrive?" she asked.

"I think around ten, but that may have changed now."

Francy slowed when she saw a Sheriff's Deputy motioning her to pull over. She stopped and rolled down her window.

She shook her head in disbelief. "Look at all the news trucks already parked. They're like vultures."

The deputy, holding clipboard, walked over to the vehicle.

"I'm Deputy Lawrence. Your name?"

"I'm Francy Baines. I'm retired from the police department."

He looked down at the list on his clipboard. "Francine Baines. Please drive ahead. An officer will direct you to parking."

"Thank you."

The deputy nodded, touching the brim of his hat. Francy rolled up the window and drove slowly ahead until she saw a familiar face pointing to a parking area.

She pulled up to where he was standing and rolled down her window.

"Hey, Pat. This looks serious," she said to the officer.

"Yeah, looks like a possible homicide. Sarge said for you to park over by the squad cars and walk down to Shep's place."

"Any idea who it is?"

"No. The body's been in the water for a while."

"Thanks. Say hello to your wife for me. Is she feeling all right?"

The officer smiled. "She's good. Baby is due in about a month."

Francy smiled and rolled up her window. She found a spot to park between two city patrol cars. She and Lainey got out and walked to the restaurant.

They could see camera crews, followed closely by reporters, carrying equipment, and hurrying to claim the best spot by the lake. An ambulance drove past them trying to dodge humans and machinery.

Behind the restaurant, two tall cranes dripped cables from their massive arms like weeping willow trees blowing in the wind. Workers in hard hats, police officers, divers, and reporters seemed to be gathered around a huge hunk of something that appeared to be partially submerged.

Francy found Sarge and she motioned for Lainey to follow her. They walked as quickly as possible over to him.

He was standing with his hands on his hips when he saw them walking toward him. He turned to meet them.

"What's happening, Sarge?" Lainey asked before Francy had a chance too.

"A young man was launching his boat around 4 a.m., trying to get a head start. Not wanting to be seen, he drove over to this spot instead of using the dock. Unfortunately, he didn't know that less than a foot from the bank, there's a steep, thirty foot drop off."

He stopped to see a young reporter and his camera man pushing people out of his way and heading directly toward him.

"I'd like a statement. Who's the corpse?" The reporter blurted out as he stuck a microphone in the officer's face.

Sarge batted the microphone away from his face and calmly, but forcefully, addressed the man.

"We have no statement. This is a restricted area." He bent his head to the left and spoke into the radio clipped to his shoulder. "Kreps. I need Media attention. Now."

"Is the Governor involved?" the obnoxious reporter questioned. "Was it murder?"

Officer Kreps arrived and quickly escorted both the reporter and his camera man away from the scene.

Sarge turned his attention back to Francy and Lainey. "When he backed the boat trailer off the bank, he heard it scrape loudly on something. The kid tried to stop and pull it back out of the water. It scraped again. He put the truck in neutral but didn't set the parking brake. The boat must have been taking on water. We think the pull on the trailer from the steep drop off and the weight of the boat caused them both to sink. And because the truck was in neutral, it followed the trailer and boat."

Francy and Lainey looked at each other and chuckled.

"You've got to be kidding. That sounds ridiculous," Francy said.

"If the kid wasn't in the truck when it went down, what body is everyone buzzing about?" Lainey asked. "And what's sticking out of the water now?"

"I'll fill you in later. Right now, I need you to find Shep and keep him under control."

"I suppose the opener is cancelled." Francy commented.

Sarge shook his head. "The Governor said it was to go on as planned." He nodded and headed over to the area where several divers were standing. Francy and Lainey fought their way through the growing crowd and around to the front of the restaurant. Every light inside was on and every table was filled. They carefully made their way through the maze of people, cameras, backpacks, and electric cords to the kitchen area. They opened the door to see Shep and four others busily preparing food and coffee.

"Mr. Morton? Can we talk with you, sir?" Lainey asked reluctantly, remembering his last comment about staying out of his kitchen.

Shep, chopping onions, looked up briefly and then continued his chopping.

"What now?" He asked.

"I know you're busy, but can we talk to you for just a moment?"

He finished the large onion he had been working on, put the pieces into a stainless steel bowl, and wiped his brow on his apron.

"I'll send the complainers to you when their food is cold." He put down his knife and cleaned his hands on a towel. "Follow me. These media idiots haven't found the backstairs yet."

He opened a side door in the kitchen and went outside. He walked a few steps then turned to face a door on his right.

"I built this addition to cover a staircase that is attached to the outside of the building. We can bring food upstairs this way and it doesn't get as cold."

He opened the door and they followed him up the stairs. At the top, he opened another door that led to the porch.

"Stand close to the building. No one will notice we're out here."

Lainey and Francy followed, being careful to stand out of the view of the growing mass of reporters below. Shep closed the door, then leaned against it.

"Sarge sent you here to babysit me, right?"

"Things around here got pretty busy this morning," Lainey said without answering his question.

"It's not the kind of news attention you thought, was it?" Francy asked.

Shep crossed his arms. "Some young kid ruined his truck and his dad's boat. What's your point?"

"You're a bright man," Lainey began. "I knew that the first time I met you. And I think under that mean, tough guy side you let people see, is a lonely man with a kind heart."

Francy stared at Lainey, then slowly moved her gaze to Shep. For a moment, his face hardened and she thought his anger might get the best of him. She steadied herself and was ready to push Lainey aside if he tried to throw a punch.

Instead, Francy saw his scowl slowly soften. He uncrossed his arms and lowered his gaze.

When he looked up, his eyes sparkled a little with tears.

"You have a good intuition," he said to Lainey. "You feel things in your gut, don't you? I do, too. I knew you had the gift. It shows in your eyes."

Startled, Lainey took a step back. "Yes, at times, I do."

"Like this morning, right?"

Her mouth opened and she couldn't hide the surprised look on her face.

"Yes. Did you feel something?"

"I have dreams. They wake me up and I'm instantly sick to my stomach," he paused to rub the back of his neck. "Last night, I saw the wreck of an old boat sitting in the middle of my restaurant with a dead man behind the steering wheel. He looked at me and said repeatedly, *"I'm not who they say I am."*

A shiver went through Francy's spine. "That's terrifying. How often do you have these dreams?"

"I never know when they are going to come."

"You didn't tell Sarge about your dream, did you?" Lainey asked even though she knew the answer.

"No. I've told the police before. At first, they considered me a suspect and I had to prove my innocence. Soon, I became known around town as a nut or phony psychic. After a while, I stopped telling anyone."

Lainey nodded and moved closer to him. She put her hand on his shoulder. "I understand. And I believe you. Sally must have believed you, too."

A single tear escaped from his eye. He wiped it away quickly.

"Sally was a wonderful woman and she suffered at times because she did believe me. I'd alert the police and a newspaper article would appear titled *"Local Nut Predicts Future"* or *"Area Crazy Man at it Again"*. Friends began avoiding her and would gossip about her about being married to me."

Shep choked back tears. Francy reached into her pocket and offered him a tissue. He smiled and nodded to thank her.

"It's okay to cry," Lainey assured him. "After my husband died, I tried to bury all those feelings of hurt and loneliness deep inside. It was eating me alive. You're safe with us. We won't tell a soul."

Francy nodded in agreement.

Shep took a deep breath in and let it out slowly.

"Thanks. Give me a second."

He walked over to the edge of the balcony and took a few more deep breaths. He turned and walked back. The tears were gone and his face wasn't quite as tense.

"Now, I've got a bunch of people to feed and I should be getting back in the kitchen. What is it you wanted from me?"

Lainey had almost forgotten why they had been sent in the first place.

"We came to see if we could help you in some way," Lainey said. "Before you go, can I ask what's sticking out of the water down there?"

"It's the hull of an old boat," Shep said quietly. "They found human remains sitting behind the steering wheel, just like I saw in the dream."

Francy gasped out loud. "Holy cow." She looked at Lainey.

"Divers think when the kid's trailer and boat went over the drop, the motor got caught on or under the helm of the sunken boat. When the crane pulled up the trailer, the sunken boat came up with it."

"My gosh. It must have been buried under more than twenty feet of water. No wonder it wasn't found before," Lainey said.

"It's common knowledge that the lake drops off at this point," Shep commented. "Nobody launches a boat from here and it's a very poor fishing spot, so no one fishes from the bank."

"Perfect spot to murder someone and sink their boat," Lainey thought aloud. She turned to Francy.

"I know. I know. You want me to talk with Sarge."

"Actually, I think we need to search the missing persons files as soon as possible," Lainey grinned.

"Let's get through this press conference, first!" Francy

laughed. "Shep, Della should be here by now. I'm sure she will help."

Shep nodded. "Is, ah, Vera coming to help?"

"Yes, she is."

"Maybe she'd be willing to help me with the coffee or something?"

Francy grinned. "You know what, I think that's a terrific idea. I'll talk with her."

An impish grin appeared on Shep's face. "Thanks."

They walked back down the stairs and into the kitchen. Shep immediately began barking orders to his staff. Lainey and Francy opened the door to the dining area. It was packed with people standing along the walls, sitting on the floor by tables, and there was a line through the front door and down the stone path.

"For Pete's sake," Francy exclaimed. "They're packed in here like sardines!"

"Let's get to the door. Della and the crew have to be here by now."

They pushed their way through the crowd and found Della standing with several officers on the porch. She was talking and waving her hands giving directions.

"I need you to clear a path so the invited guests and Governor can at least get inside the restaurant," she instructed. She looked up to see the two walking toward her and motioned to them.

"You'd think Captain Picard and the Enterprise had landed in Mirror Falls!" she spouted.

"It snowballed out of control, that's for sure," Francy replied.

"Can you help the officers clear these people standing around the outside of the restaurant? I need all of them to go back behind the barrier. I've gotten word that the head cheese man should be arriving in less than an hour."

"Call Sarge. He'll get his guys moving," Lainey suggested.

"He's preoccupied and I hate to bug him with more. Francy, can you do anything?"

"I'll do what I can. But I think you'd better alert Sarge that the Governor will be here soon."

"I will. Paul is back there with him now. It's his funeral home's turn to handle the body."

Before Lainey could say anything, Della was being paged with a different problem.

She answered the radio and listened to the newest urgent issue.

"I'll do what I can, but I'm not in charge of making sure the bathrooms have toilet paper!"

She rolled her eyes and Lainey laughed.

"If I *ever* volunteer for this again, shoot me!" she sighed.

CHAPTER 5

Della went inside and suggested that Sarge's men started corralling the people and herd them into their designated seating or standing areas. Lainey stayed on the porch, partially to keep from being trampled. She wanted to be able to run for Sarge if Francy and the officers needed help moving the mass of people off the lawn.

For a few minutes, the lawn and parking lot resembled a huge mosh pit. People were jumping up and down to get a view of the recovery scene. Some were yelling and waving their hands for more equipment, and a line of cars with impatient drivers honking their horns trying to find a place to park.

It'll be a miracle if this gets organized in time.

Lainey looked at her watch. If Della's reports were correct, the Governor would be driving up, expecting to be the main attraction, in twenty-five minutes.

She moved her gaze back to the chaos in front of her and saw a small open space appear on the stone pathway. She watched as the opening became wider and longer. At the same time, the cars jammed in the parking lot receded back into the side streets.

Della walked out of the restaurant, looking at Lainey. "He's going to be here in ten minutes. How's it going?"

"It was like Moses waving his staff and parting the Red Sea," Lainey said in amazement. "The police moved a few people and voila! The crowds are where they should be and the parking area in front is empty, waiting for the Governor's limo."

"Same thing happened inside. The mayor took the microphone and started giving commands. People listened to him for once."

"That's a first!" Lainey laughed. "Melvin Jackson isn't a forceful personality. He has a hard time running the city council meetings."

"He must have eaten his Wheaties this morning because he roared like Tony the Tiger."

"That's Frosted Flakes, not Wheaties."

"Whatever. He must have had a double portion!"

Della's radio sounded with a general message.

"The limo has turned off Hwy 71. Please advise all unit stations. Arrival in under a minute."

Della looked at Lainey. "Better get ready to check ID's - but I think most of the media is already in your section."

Lainey nodded. "Let's get the show on the road!"

She walked over to the media area. They had heard the radio announcement and were standing, readying their cameras for the Governor's big entrance.

"You must stay behind the roped barrier or you will be escorted out the back door," she said loudly. One of the officers standing by the front door came over and barked the same instructions.

"They'll crowd the rope. We have two more guys coming to make sure no one goes underneath it," the officer said.

"Thanks. I appreciate the help."

Lainey turned to watch the front door and the entourage that would precede in before the Governor. The political parade began with several local bankers, business owners, and perhaps the community's most famous native, Marvin Jackson, a former University of Minnesota Gopher football quarterback who happened to be the Mayor's son.

State Representatives followed with the Mayor at the end. Once they were seated, the cameras turned back to the door to await the governor's entrance.

Lainey watched as two bodyguards entered first. When they were satisfied that all was clear, they motioned for the Governor. Her heart raced when she saw Raymond Sullivan walk in ahead of the Governor. Raymond smiled and winked at her as if he still had feelings for her. Instantly, the searing pain she had worked so hard to overcome, pierced her soul once more.

Stop it! Shake him off. Don't let him hurt you again.

She hadn't noticed that the Governor walked past and was standing at the podium in the front of the dining room. Raymond was on his right and the Mayor on his left.

Cameras clicked rapidly, sounding like a hundred clocks loudly ticking. The Governor tapped the microphone on the podium and motioned for the audience to sit. The media area didn't obey.

Lainey turned to the officer standing beside her. He nodded and quietly motioned for the other officers to get their attention. He batted the air with his hands as if he were pushing something down. The other officers nodded and began getting the media's attention. Reluctantly, the reporters sat while the people holding the television cameras stood at the back of the section.

Lainey moved closer to the aisle so she could see the podium. She dug out a piece of paper from her pants pocket and was ready to jot down the names of the lucky few who would sit in the Governor's boat. She tried hard not to look at Raymond.

"It's my honor to welcome you to this year's fishing opener. I want to thank Mirror Falls, the City Council, and Mayor Jackson for organizing this event. And thank you to the many volunteers who have tirelessly planned…" the Governor's statement was cut short by a rogue reporter who stood up and yelled a question.

"What's the name of the body found in the boat? Are you involved in the murder?" The same reporter that had confronted Sarge earlier was now badgering the Governor. "Why didn't…"

Two police officers grabbed the reporter before he could finish his sentence and hastily took him out of the room. The commotion started a barrage of questions from others that quickly grew into a roar. The Governor looked over the crowd. He raised his hands and shouted in the microphone.

"Please! Please! Sit down. I won't address that question until you're quiet."

He repeated the command several times before the crowd settled down.

"I'm only going to say this once and I will not take any further questions on this matter."

Sarge had walked up to stand beside the three at the podium and the two bodyguards were standing behind the Governor.

"We are all saddened at the discovery this morning. We will make every effort to work with law enforcement. At this time, I will defer to Officer Ben Sargent."

Sarge walked up to the microphone and put his hands on the sides of the podium. He surveyed the room before he spoke.

"At approximately 4:30 a.m. this morning, we received a

call concerning a pickup truck, boat trailer, and boat that was underwater. The caller had attempted to launch his boat from a restricted area instead of the approved ramp. The site has a large drop off less than twelve inches from the bank. The trailer, boat still attached, fell into the lake and the force of the drop took the pickup with it."

Sarge paused as he saw the media raise their hands almost in unison.

"Our recovery efforts to pull the pickup, trailer, and boat were successful. However, the boat apparently became tangled with an object when it sank. That object was pulled out of the water, still attached to the boat and trailer. This is an ongoing investigation. We have no more details at this time."

Sarge moved away from the podium as reporters began shouting out questions. The Mayor stepped up to the microphone.

"He said no questions. This press conference is to draw names for a chance to sit in the Governor's boat. If you don't quiet down, you will be removed from this building!"

The Mayor backed away from the microphone as a stunned silence fell over the room. No one had ever heard Melvin Jackson speak with such authority or anger. The local business officials looked at each other and shrugged their shoulders. Even the Governor was shocked.

"Thank you, Mayor," the Governor said as he once again stood in front of the microphone. "Now, let's move on."

He grinned and tried to act as if nothing out of the ordinary had occurred. He turned to Raymond Sullivan.

"Everyone is familiar with Raymond Sullivan. He has graciously agreed to be our Master of Ceremonies. I'll turn the microphone over to him. Please give him a hand."

Raymond smiled; ever the poised, handsome businessman, and stood in front of the podium. The sparse clapping ended quickly.

"Thank you, Governor. I'm honored to join you, the Mayor, and the wonderful people of Mirror Falls for this first ever official drawing. I also join you in the concern over the unfortunate event this morning."

Raymond paused briefly, nodding to the Governor and Sarge.

"For those who might not be familiar with our fishing opener traditions, allow me to briefly explain the importance of this drawing."

Raymond told how the fishing opener signaled the beginning of spring and the end of the long winter. He described the important economic impact communities felt with the return of tourism. Finally, he came to the tradition of being allowed to fish in the Governor's boat.

"Over the years, fishing tales grew, as sometimes the size of the fish in the story grew, too." A chuckle rippled across the room. "These helped create the folklore that to fish in the Governor's boat gave that person luck and brought bigger fish to their lines."

The mood in the room had lightened as Raymond skillfully guided them.

"In an attempt to be fair to all anglers, a new way of choosing the six who would fish with the Governor was suggested this year. Each entrant's name was put in a large fishing tackle box." He reached underneath the podium and produce a large red tackle box. He turned the front toward audience.

"I want you to see that it is locked. Last evening, a random person from Mirror Falls was asked to put the entries in the tackle box and lock it. They gave the key to Sarge, who hasn't let it out of his sight."

He looked at Sarge who nodded. Raymond motioned for

him to step forward and the two of them walked in front of the podium, the tackle box still facing the crowd.

Sarge took the key from his shirt pocket and unlocked the tackle box. He put the key back in his pocket.

"Before I ask Ben to open the box, I want to make sure you all see that I have nothing up my sleeves!" The crowd laughed as he raised his sleeves, wiggled his fingers, and then proceeded to pull out his pants pockets to show they were empty.

"Everyone satisfied?" he asked the crowd.

There was a general *yes* and Raymond smiled.

"Officer, please open the tackle box."

Sarge had a solemn look on his face trying to keep the mood Raymond had worked hard to setup. He opened the box.

"Mr. Sullivan, would you please draw out the first name." Sarge commanded.

Raymond nodded reverently and put his hand inside. He turned his face to the audience and closed his eyes. Then he ran his hand back and forth in the tackle box as if striving to find the choice entry. The crowd applauded and laughed.

Suddenly his hand stopped. His eyebrows raised, eyes still closed, and a big smile appeared on his face. He slowly raised his hand to show the one strip of paper it held. The crowd grew silent.

He opened his eyes and looked at his hand.

"Please hand the ticket to Mayor Jackson," Sarge instructed, trying to keep a straight face.

Raymond nodded and with his hand held out in front of him, walked over to the mayor. He almost bowed when he presented his hand to the Mayor. The Mayor nodded and took the paper.

"Mayor Jackson, would you please read the name on the piece of paper," Sarge said.

The Mayor looked at the paper, then looked up, then looked back at the paper.

"It's blank," he shouted.

Angry cries from the audience erupted immediately.

"It's a setup!"

"What a crock!"

"You're as crooked as the Governor!"

There was an alarmed looked on Sarge's face as he quickly studied the audience, looking to see where his officers were stationed.

The Mayor raise his hand and shouted, "I'm kidding! I'm kidding! Hold your horses!"

Confused, the crowd's shouts turned to moans.

"Read the darn name, Jackson." Someone shouted out in frustration.

"Okay! I was just teasing." He looked once more at the name.

"The first lucky winner is Charlie Crowfoot!"

Lainey gasped.

Charlie Crowfoot? Oh, no. Not bait-shop Charlie!"

Some in the group applauded and some in the group groaned. Raymond, Sarge and the Mayor repeated the process five more times. Each time a name was read, some cheered, some sneered.

The name drawing event took a total of ten minutes. That was it. The order in which the dignitaries had entered, reversed as they exited. The entire recessional took less than five minutes. The crowd of media and reporters evacuated the restaurant as if they were running from a tornado.

Lainey stood, watching the people disappear, and wondered where Francy and Della were. Within a half hour, the restaurant was emptied and only a few locals remained. She saw Della coming toward her through the kitchen door.

Francy followed closely behind. She met them in the middle of the once crowded room. Trash was littered everywhere.

"Look at the mess they left behind," Della said. "It'll take hours to clean this up."

Francy nodded. "People can be real slobs sometimes. We see it all the time at community concerts and such."

"What I can't believe is the tremendous amount of security, volunteers, workers, and the money spent on this. It took less than ten minutes to draw those names!" Lainey was clearly frustrated.

Della nodded. "Did you hear the first name?"

Lainey rolled her eyes. "Can you believe it?"

"We were in the kitchen when Shep heard it," Francy stated. "Good thing Mom was there to calm him down."

Lainey's mouth opened wide. "Calm him? Vera? She called him an old goat."

"Well, sometimes, one old goat doesn't smell as bad once the *other* old goat learns the hay he had to eat was rotten," Francy smiled.

CHAPTER 6

As they walked toward the kitchen door, Shep and Vera walked out of it. They were in deep conversation and didn't see the ladies walking toward them. Vera turned to face him when they had cleared the door.

"Shep, I told you. Charlie didn't cheat. There is no way he put a hundred entries in the tackle box with his name on them."

"I don't know how he did it, but I'll figure it out. He cheated, pure and simple."

Vera rolled her eyes and shook her head. "You're as stubborn as a donkey!"

"Maybe so. He's cheated me before and you know it."

"That was years ago. Water under the bridge. He explained what happened and Sally understood. Why can't you let it go?"

Shep frowned and turned his gaze toward the ladies who were now standing behind Vera, trying hard to hide the smiles on their faces.

"The Whoopee group is waiting to talk with you," he said to Vera. "Guess I've provided enough comic relief for the moment." He nodded as he walked past the ladies and out the front door.

Vera turned to face the group. "That man! He infuriates me at times!"

The three ladies couldn't hold their laughter any longer.

"He thinks the box had a hundred slips of paper with Charlie's name on it?" Francy tried to ask through her chuckles.

"That's the funniest thing I've heard," Della laughed. "I know for a fact that he had only one entry, like every other angler."

"Trying to convince him is like pulling the teeth out of a laughing hyena's mouth with a spoon!" Vera stated bluntly.

Lainey laughed out loud. "Well, if anyone can make him change his mind, you can, Vera. I think he's a bit fond of you."

"Piddle! He's an old sour puss!"

"We're going outside to find Sarge. Mom, want to come with us?" Francy asked.

"Sure. I persuaded Shep to let me take some cookies he made yesterday to the guys working out back. I'll grab them and follow you."

They nodded and walked into the kitchen. Vera picked up the tray of cookies left out on the counter. They walked out the back door and headed toward Sarge, who was talking with the men working the cranes. He saw them and hastily finished his conversation. Turning to face the ladies, he raised his right hand as if to motion them to stop.

"Before you ask any questions, I don't have any information I can share."

"Now, Ben Sargent," Vera began in a voice that sounded like a mother scolding her child. "I brought cookies for these poor men who have been working for hours out here. Surely they can take a short break to eat them."

Sarge's expression softened and he nodded in approval.

"Shep said you were bringing them. It's been an exceedingly long morning for many of the guys. I'm sure they will appreciate them."

"They're Shep's famous gooey German chocolate nuggets with extra dark chocolate chips," Vera grinned as she handed the tray to Sarge, then leaned close to his shoulder. "I know where he hides the dough if you need me to bake more!"

Sarge grinned. "I think this will be enough." He walked over to a picnic table and set the tray of goodies down. He motioned for the group of workers standing on the bank to take a break.

While Sarge was dispensing the cookies, Lainey walked over to a large tarp that appeared to be covering the unknown sunken boat. She bent down to raise one edge of the tarp.

What kind of boat are you? Who murdered your driver?

"I've heard you're the nosey investigator that helps Sarge," a deep male voice whispered behind her.

Startled, she dropped the edge of the tarp quickly and turned to face the voice. It was Marvin Jackson.

"Oh, uhm, you startled me," Lainey stuttered trying to regain her composure. "You didn't leave with your dad?"

"I came out here to see if I could lend a hand. Curious about what's under the tarp?"

There was no response.

Marvin Jackson walked around Lainey to the other side of the boat so he'd be facing her.

He knows what boat this is. He's taunting me...

"I'm sure Sarge can fill you in on any details he wants you to know," he said, running his hand over the top of the tarp. "Until then, I guess you would say the information is *confidential*."

Lainey nodded slightly, careful not to blink as she stared

directly into his eyes. There was a moment of silence as their eyes locked, each one daring the other to speak.

"Hey, Marvin," Francy's voiced broke the tension in the air. "Did you want to speak with Sarge? Della can radio him for you."

Marvin smiled. "No need. I'll talk with him on my way out." He nodded to Lainey and Francy, offering a fake salute as he walked toward the picnic table.

"Did you see the arrogant smirk he tried to pass off as a smile?" Francy commented. "He's his father's son, that's for sure."

"Why does he care about the boat under this tarp? Wonder what he knows? And I wonder why Sarge…"

"Wonder why I did what?" Sarge said, cutting her off in mid-sentence. He had seen Marvin and Lainey standing by the tarp. When he saw Francy move in their direction, he followed behind sensing there might be trouble.

"Oh, Sarge," Lainey mumbled. "I was… I mean we were chatting with Marvin Jackson." She looked nervously at Francy.

"That's right," Francy added. "He must have been helping with the investigation."

Sarge pursed his lips and raised one eyebrow. "It's been a long day and I don't want to play twenty questions. Get to your point."

Lainey frowned and let out a big sigh. "We've worked together too long, Sarge. You know me too well."

"What happened between you and Jackson?"

"Lainey wanted to look under the tarp and Marvin stopped her," Francy explained. "You know we can help you with this investigation."

Francy was standing with her hands on her hips while Lainey leaned against the tarp-covered boat. Sarge studied the two ladies for several minutes before he spoke.

"What exactly did Marvin say?" he finally asked. "What did you say to him?"

Lainey rolled her eyes, then stood up from leaning on the boat. "I was looking under the tarp when he walked up behind me. It startled me. Other than calling me nosey, he said to speak with you about any details."

"Nosey was probably not the best choice of words," he replied slowly. "And your response to that was?"

"Nothing. I said nothing."

He nodded. "Is that what you heard, Francy?"

"Yes, sir."

Sarge sighed. "Mayor Jackson wanted Marvin to remain on scene as his representative. I had no say in the matter."

"Did he see the boat? Or the body?" Lainey asked.

"Paul had removed the remains from the boat and taken them to the county coroner's office before Marvin appeared. But, yes, he did see the boat."

"Can we see it? Or…" Lainey began.

"Go to the office. The pictures are there. Things are beginning to settle down a little bit and the actual opener begins in a few hours. I still have a great deal to get done."

He smiled, but exhaustion from the day's event was evident on his face. His eyes were bloodshot and puffy, dark circles were forming underneath them.

"I need to get back. Francy, I'll call the station and let them know to give you and Lainey access to the files for the pictures," he said. "And make sure Della gives her radio to one of my officers before you leave."

"Thanks, Sarge," Lainey replied. "We know the pressure you're under. We will help if we can."

"Thanks, sir," Francy added. "I'll let you know if we find anything."

Sarge turned to walk toward the last remaining crane operator. He took a few steps, then turned around to face them again and said, "Tell Vera to thank Shep for the cookies."

"Will do," Lainey said. She turned to face Francy, looking back toward the restaurant. "We need to get in touch with Paul immediately. Where's Della?"

"She and Mom are standing by the picnic table."

Lainey nodded and the two walked over to where a group of officers were devouring the last of the gooey nuggets.

"These were delicious, Mrs. Abernathy," one of the officers said as he took the last crumbs off the tray.

"Shep's recipe," Vera answered. "I'll tell him how much you enjoyed them."

"I see the cookies were a big hit, Mom," Francy said as she and Lainey walked up beside her.

"He uses Sally's recipe, you know," Vera replied. "But, yes, these were very good."

"What was going on with you and Marvin?" Della asked. "I've been watching and listening to see if I could hear anything over the radio."

"We'll fill you in later. Right now, Sarge needs you to turn in the radio and we need to find Paul," Francy said.

"Paul should be back at work," Della replied. "I'll call and make sure he's there."

"Sounds good. I'm not sure where everyone parked, so let's meet at Babe's House of Caffeine. It'll be nice to have coffee and get our ducks in a row before going to the station." Lainey suggested.

"Meet you in thirty minutes," Francy said. "Mom and I will drop off the tray in the kitchen and head that way."

"Well, uhm, actually," Vera said a bit awkwardly. "Shep asked me to stay for a little bit. He spilled water on an old recipe he's been using and the writing faded out. He asked if I could help him decipher the ingredients."

"Oh, really," Francy grinned. "And he can't remember these ingredients?"

"Now don't you go jumping to conclusions, young lady," Vera cautioned as her face flushed just a little. "I didn't like this particular recipe and I'm sure we can change the ingredients to make it better."

Della and Lainey exchanged glances and smiled.

"I see," Francy said as her grin widened. "Remember that curfew is 10 p.m."

"Very funny," Vera snapped. "Your Dad's curfew kept you out of trouble, Francine Abernathy Baines. And I don't need to be reminded of a curfew!"

"Okay, okay," Francy laughed. "Call if you need something."

Della and Lainey chuckled out loud.

"We love you," Della said putting her arm around Vera.

"You girls get going," Vera grinned. "And don't get into any trouble without me!"

"We wouldn't dare," Lainey smiled.

Vera picked up the empty tray and headed to the kitchen. Francy and Lainey walked to the parking lot to find their cars while Della found Sarge and returned the radio.

Lainey found her car, and when she was safely inside, she stretched, yawned, and then sat back in the seat before starting the engine. Her mind was churning with possibilities, motives, and questions about the body found in the boat.

"I need a large mocha frappe with a turkey and cheese club sandwich," she said aloud as she started the car. "And I think I'll splurge on a bag of sour cream and onion chips, too."

Francy was getting out of her car in front of Babe's when Lainey arrived. She parked in the space behind her friend's car. As she got out, she double checked that it was locked.

Francy was holding the door open and the two walked into the familiar coffee shop, looking for one of their favorite tables.

"Let's sit towards the back so we can talk freely," Francy said. She motioned to Marie, their usual waitress, to show her which table they would be using.

The two sat down at one of the high top tables in the back and took off their coats.

"Hey, ladies," Marie said as she walked toward them. "It's not a regular Whoopee night, is it?"

"Hello, Marie," Lainey answered. "No, we've been working the fishing opener and thought we needed some decent coffee and food."

Marie nodded. "Just the two of you?"

"Della will be coming shortly," Francy replied.

"And Vera?"

"Mom had a previous engagement," Francy said, trying not to laugh. She looked at Lainey who was grinning widely.

"I'll come back to take your order when Della arrives," the waitress said.

"Sounds good. Thanks, Marie," Lainey said.

When the waitress was a safe distance away, Francy leaned forward on the table and laughed.

"Stop grinning! I was trying to keep a straight face!" she sputtered.

Lainey chuckled loudly. "I know, I couldn't help it. Vera and Shep on a recipe date?" They looked at each other and laughed.

"You two still laughing about Vera and her date?" Della asked as she walked up to the table. Her husband, Paul, followed behind her with a look of complete confusion.

"What date? Vera has a date? With whom?" Paul asked innocently.

The three ladies stopped chuckling, looked at each other, then burst out in laughter once again.

"It's a long story, dear. I'll fill you in later," Della answered, trying to catch her breath.

Paul shrugged. He knew better than to try and ask the group his question again. Della's cue for him to hush was always *I'll fill you in later*. He'd find out the scoop at home.

Marie came to their table, took their orders, and had their food back to them in a short time.

Lainey took a big bite out of her club sandwich. "I didn't realize how hungry I was. This tastes so good!"

"Me, too," Francy said. "I love their tomato bisque soup."

Paul and Della split a large oriental chicken salad and were busy dividing it up between their plates. Lainey watched as Della picked out all of the onions, peppers, and a small portion of lettuce to put on her plate. She carefully left all the chicken, croutons, and most of the salad on Paul's plate.

Paul noticed the puzzled look on Lainey's face. "She thinks she's helping me to eat a healthy diet." He motioned to Marie to bring him a second strawberry malt, then turned to Lainey and grinned. "So I can have seconds."

Lainey and Francy laughed. Della shook her head and said, "You're not helping!"

After they had finished eating, Paul was the first one to talk about the incident that morning.

"Della says you want to know about the remains," he began. "I can't tell you much. The body is at the county coroner's office. It will take a couple of days to get any identification."

"Do you think it *can* be identified? I mean, has it been underwater too long?" Lainey asked.

"We use the latest technology for DNA testing. I'm

hopeful some identification will be found. I've seen remains in worse condition and they were identified."

Della shivered. "I could not do that kind of work. Autopsies give me the creeps."

"I know you saw the body, Paul," Francy said. "Got any idea of male or female? Or how long it might have been dead?"

He shook his head. "I didn't have a chance to examine the remains. With the media presence all around, Sarge wanted me to go to the coroner's office as quickly as possible."

"But you must have some idea?" Lainey prodded. "A gut feeling perhaps?"

Paul grinned. "We've been friends for over ten years now," he looked at Della and smiled. "If I had to guess, I'd say it was male. But that is strictly a guess at this point."

Francy leaned back in her chair. "We're going to the station to look at photos of the boat. I hope they took several before they removed the body."

"I'm sure they did. They didn't move anything before the coroner arrived." Paul replied.

"How come the body didn't float up after a time?" Lainey asked. "Did it get stuck in the boat? How did the boat sink? Did you see a gaping hole in the hull?"

Paul took his time answering. "I'm sure you have many questions that the pictures will answer." He hesitated and thought carefully before he spoke again.

"A body can't float if it's anchored to the boat."

CHAPTER 7

Francy's jaw dropped as she looked at Lainey. "You were right! It was murder!"

Lainey nodded and winked. "I had a feeling it was."

"Don't jump to conclusions," Paul cautioned. "There are too many unknown factors to immediately deduce it was murder. Look at the photos and wait for the coroner's report."

Della wiggled in her chair. "Can you at least give us an idea of how long that body was under water? I know you have a guess." She leaned closer to Paul, put her hand on his arm, and blew him a kiss.

"Flirting with me to get information is husband bribery!" he grinned. "You're not playing fair."

"Everything's fair in love and war, dear." She batted her eyes playfully.

Paul rolled his eyes and laughed. "If I had to guess," and he looked directly at Lainey, "and I mean *guess*, I'd say at least forty years."

Francy raised her eyebrows. "Wow, that's a long time for someone to be missing."

Lainey agreed. "Maybe this person wasn't reported as missing? We need to get to the police station."

"I'm going to ride home with Paul," Della said. "I'll look online for missing persons or boating accidents and see if anything comes up."

"That would be terrific," Francy said. "We'll give you a call later."

The four paid their bills and said their goodbyes. Lainey and Francy walked quickly to their cars.

"I'll follow you," Lainey said as she got into her car.

"Sounds good. Let's park in the back of the station." Francy replied.

The drive to the station took less than five minutes but trying to find a parking spot in the crowded backlot took much longer.

"You can tell it's the fishing opener night," Francy said as she got out of her car and locked it. "All officers on duty park their personal cars back here."

Lainey shut her car door, making sure it was locked. "I don't remember this lot ever being full."

The two walked quickly toward the large metal door at the back of the police station. Francy punched in her code and looked up toward a camera lens that was placed above the door.

"Hello, Francy," a voice said over the intercom. "I'll open the door for you."

"Thanks. Sarge should have told you we were coming."

"It's been remarkably busy here," the voice responded, "when you hear the click of the door, come on in."

Francy nodded as a loud click came from the door. She quickly grabbed the handle and opened the door. She motioned for Lainey to go through first, then followed. The door slammed closed shortly after the two walked inside and a hallway motion light came on.

Lainey blinked a few times as her eyes adjusted to the brightness of the ceiling lights. She followed Francy down the hall until she stopped at the last door on the right. There wasn't a sign on the door.

"Let's use the computer in the dungeon," Francy said as she punched in her code to open the door. "The pictures should be downloaded on it."

The lights came on automatically as they entered the room. The dungeon was the name the officers had given to the evidence room years ago. There were no windows and only the one door. The few parts of the cement walls that could be seen between the rows of tall metal shelving were a dingy white and covered with scuff marks and scratches. The shelves were packed with cardboard boxes. A large computer monitor and a silver lamp were the only things on the metal desk that occupied one corner of the room. It was surrounded on three sides by file cabinets, some black, some grey. Each cabinet had five drawers. The only other furniture in the room was a desk chair and a tall wooden stool. Both were behind the desk.

"I can see why they call this the dungeon," Lainey said as she sat down on the stool. "It smells like dirty socks in here."

"Some of this stuff is decades old. I haven't worked back here in years, but you never forget the smell," Francy said as she sat down in front of the computer. "Let's see those pictures."

Lainey scooted the stool closer to get a clearer view of the screen. Francy punched in a few codes, opened a few file folders, and within a few minutes, had access to the photos they wanted.

"These aren't categorized yet, but we can see the time each was taken and put them in order from that," Francy said. "Remember it was dark when these were taken. Here we go."

The first picture showed the pickup truck with the trailer but cut off before the boat on the trailer was shown.

"I'm sure this was taken to get the license plate of the truck. The next one should show the boat that was on the trailer," Francy remarked.

The next picture did show the boat on the trailer, with its motor clearly stuck in the front of the sunken boat.

Lainey leaned closer to the screen. "Is that motor stuck in the hull?"

"I'm not sure if it's the hull or some sort of railing," Francy replied. "Let's find pictures of the boat and the body."

The next few pictures were of the operation, getting the submerged boat onto the shore and the many workers and officers that were assisting.

Suddenly, the screen filled with a picture of the entire sunken boat. The body was leaning against the left side of the steering wheel.

"Can you increase the size of this picture?" Lainey asked. "Paul said the body was anchored to the boat. Can we see that?"

Francy resized the picture and she and Lainey grimaced at the closer view of the deceased. The skeleton had one boney wrist that was attached to the steering wheel.

"Oh, my gosh!" Lainey sat back and looked at Francy. "It was handcuffed. No wonder it didn't surface."

"Is that a piece of clothing hanging on that handcuff?" Francy asked.

Lainey stared at the screen. "It could be. I'm going to ask Sarge when I see him tomorrow."

"Wait," Francy said as she scrolled over the photo. "Do those look like bricks to you?"

Scattered around the skeleton appeared to be cement bricks. Lainey rubbed her chin.

"Boy, it sure does. Can we find more pictures of the boat? There has to be something that caused it to sink."

Francy opened several more photos until she found two that showed each side of the sunken boat. The left side showed nothing other than rust, mud, and algae. But the right side showed much more.

"Do you see that?" Lainey said excitedly. "I think those are letters!"

Francy zoomed in on the side of the boat. "It's a name all right. Looks like *A Gemelos Dream*."

"I've never heard that word, but I'll do some research and see what it means," Lainey said. "Do you see any holes in the boat?"

"I can't see any. Let me see if there is any kind of report on file."

Lainey continued to look at the boat name. "Most boat names are kind of funny or cute, you know? Wonder what a Gemelos is?"

"I'm afraid there is no report filed," Francy said as she leaned back in the chair. "Most likely they haven't had time with the fishing opener."

"True. Can you do a Google search with this computer?"

"Not this one, why?"

"I'd like to search newspaper articles or clippings for the name Gemelos," Lainey answered. "I know it's getting late and it's been a long day. Why don't we plan to meet in the morning? We could meet for breakfast over at the 66 Truck Stop diner."

"Sounds good. What time?"

"If Della comes, we should plan on 9 a.m."

"That'll be early for her!" Francy laughed.

"I'll text her and let her know. Maybe she's found something about a missing person."

They shut down the computer, left the room and headed out to the rear parking lot.

"Thanks, Francy," Lainey said as she opened her car door. "I'm so glad you were a dispatcher!"

"No problem. Glad to help. Guess I'd better head home to see if Mom has made it back from her date with Shep."

"I forgot about that!" Lainey laughed. "My dad used to watch from the front window and flip the porch light off and on when it was time for me to come in the house. Maybe you could try that with your mom!"

"She'd throw a fit for sure," Francy chuckled. "See you in the morning."

They got in their cars and drove out of the parking lot, each heading to their own homes. Lainey turned her radio volume up when a John Denver song came on. She loved his singing and it seemed to calm her. It wasn't long before she was inside her house, sitting in her recliner with her cat, Powie, on her lap. She yawned a few times and fell asleep in the chair.

Please, help me! I'm not who they say I am. Help me! I'm not who they say I am... I'M NOT WHO THEY SAY I AM... HELP ME!

Lainey awoke suddenly with a gasp. Her heart was pounding in her chest and she felt sick to her stomach. She looked around to see who had been talking to her. Then she realized she had been dreaming. She felt a chill go through her as she remembered the vision Shep had shared with her.

I saw the wreck of an old boat sitting in my restaurant with a dead man behind the steering wheel. He looked at me and said over and over again, I'm not who they say I am.

She took a few deep breaths to gather her composure and walked into her office to turn on her computer.

"There must be something in a news article about a missing person," she said aloud. "But where to start?"

For the next couple of hours, Lainey searched the internet for anything that might provide a clue to a boat disappearance or accident. She found a couple of articles in The Weekly Drip, a rogue area newspaper that was known for airing gossip and the dirty laundry of locals. Two cars driven into a lake by drunk teens, old rumors of affairs of people who had been deceased for years, but nothing on a sunken boat.

"Let's see what Google has to say about the word gemelos," she said to the computer screen. As soon as she hit enter, everything she ever wanted to know about the word was right in front of her.

Sometimes I LOVE the internet!

She clicked on a few of the links, and as the pages printed, she noticed the time on the screen read 7:30 a.m. She quickly saved the search, turned off her computer, and stapled the printed pages together. She put them on the counter beside her iPad and headed to the bedroom to get ready for her meeting with Della and Francy.

Lainey liked to be early for any meeting. She felt it gave her an edge and allowed her time to observe the people or the place of the meeting. She arrived at the 66 Diner a half hour early and asked for a booth near a front window. As she sat down, she saw Francy pull up and, to her surprise, Vera was with her.

"Morning you two," Lainey said as Francy and Vera entered the diner. "You're up early, Vera. How was your evening?"

"Fine."

There was an awkward silence that followed. Lainey

could tell by the look of frustration on Francy's face that they had been arguing about something.

Vera took off her coat and slid in the booth opposite of Lainey. Usually, Francy would sit next to her. But this morning, she asked for a chair and sat at the edge of the table.

"Okay, what's going on between you two?" Lainey asked.

Vera shrugged her shoulders and looked out the window.

"Mom got home at 3:35 this morning," Francy stated flatly. "But her car arrived around 6:30."

"What? Vera, were you in an accident?" Lainey asked.

Vera stared out the window and did not respond.

"Oh, no." Francy said flipping her hand in front of her face. "There was no accident. It appears Mom's car was used as a getaway vehicle. The police brought it back after their investigation."

Lainey's mouth flew open. "Holy cow!" She looked at Vera. "What in the world did you do?"

Still no response.

Francy leaned back in her chair and winked at Lainey. "Mom's got a criminal record now."

Vera turned, glared at Francy, and said sternly, "I... we don't have a criminal record. The charges were dropped."

Lainey raised her hands and shrugged. "What happened? What charges? I thought you were baking cookies with Shep."

"Oh, they were baking more than cookies," Francy said, trying hard not to smile. "They were making a new batch of stink bait."

Vera snorted and crossed her arms in frustration. "It was Shep's idea, that darn old goat!"

"Stink bait? You were arrested for making stink bait?"

Vera rolled her eyes. "No. Anyone can make stink bait."

"Remember the feud between Shep and Charlie Crowfoot?" Francy began. "Well, this is a continuation of that story from all those years ago."

Francy leaned forward and began telling the story of the incident between Shep and Charlie. They had grown up together as friends, worked together on their family farms, and had started a little side business selling homemade stink bait. They'd developed a secret recipe for the bait and were doing pretty well selling it to local anglers.

Then Sally Ervin moved to town. She was beautiful, funny, and planned to open a new restaurant in Mirror Falls. Shep and Charlie were both smitten. Sally dated both of them but fell head over heels in love with Shep. They married and opened the Backwater Restaurant.

Charlie was hurt and angry but said nothing to Shep or Sally. The two still met regularly to make their stink bait concoction. Since they bowled on the same team, the two decided to host a tournament and give away a prize of free stink bait for one lucky angler to be used during that year's fishing opener. They had hoped it would be publicity for their business.

Shortly before the tournament, Sally became ill. She went to the Mayo Clinic and was diagnosed with breast cancer. Shep was devastated but dropped everything to be by her side and supported her through the treatments. He closed the restaurant for a while. She did marvelously well and after a year, she was given a clean bill of health.

Della arrived while Francy was telling the story. She sat down beside Vera, took hold of her hand, and listened.

The waitress came and they ordered coffee and their breakfasts.

"Francy, how does Sally's cancer play a part of this feud?" Lainey asked.

"The man who won the stink bait prize owned a chain of sporting goods stores around the Twin Cities area. He loved the stink bait and wanted to stock it in all his stores. Shep was out of pocket tending to Sally, so the man spoke with Charlie."

Vera cleared her throat and put her hands on the table. "Charlie took credit for the bait recipe and signed a lucrative contract to be the sole supplier for the stores. Shep and Sally received nothing. Lord knows they could have used the income to pay doctor's bills. And Shep could no longer use that recipe. Charlie has made money on that for years."

"I understand. Hence the feud that continues," Lainey said. "But how does this involve Vera driving a getaway car?"

Della laughed and squeezed Vera's hand. "Paul heard the call on his police scanner this morning. Seems Shep and Vera were trying to break into Charlie's Bait Shop!"

Lainey paused, then laughed out loud. "Are you kidding me? You're bait shop burglars?"

The three ladies laughed, but Vera did not.

"As I said, it was Shep's idea and…"

"And you agreed?" Della asked, still chuckling loudly.

Vera took in a deep breath and let it out slowly. "All we planned to do was replace some of Charlie's stink bait supply with…," she paused as if finding the right words, "a different recipe."

"Different recipe my foot!" Francy grinned. "Shep had ground up fish bones, canned dog food, dill pickle relish, and cayenne pepper to put in place of the stink bait! No one could catch fish with that."

Lainey laughed in spite of herself. "All because Charlie was chosen to sit in the Governor's boat?"

"Exactly. If the Governor didn't catch fish, and since Charlie was chosen to supply all the bait, he would get the blame for an unsuccessful opener." Francy concluded.

"None of this would have occurred if Charlie hadn't come over to Shep yesterday bragging about *his* great stink bait recipe," Vera began. "I saw the hurt and anger in Shep's eyes and with Sally being gone, I did what she would have done to help him."

A light bulb went off in Lainey's head. "Vera, Shep made the bait in that small, back kitchen, didn't he? The one that said *Shep and Sally* on the door?"

Vera's eyes widened. "How do you know about that room?"

"I stumbled across it early yesterday."

"Yes, that's where he makes his own stink bait. He has plans to try and market his own brand one day."

"So, you drove Shep over to Charlie's and waited in your car while he broke in to exchange the bait." Della stated.

"He didn't *break* in, the back door was open. We didn't realize Charlie was in the shed behind of the shop. I guess he saw us and called the police."

"They took Mom and Shep to the station and waited for Charlie to come to sign the paperwork. Luckily, he decided not to press charges," Francy said. "My friend from the station called me to come take *Boris and Natasha* home."

Della and Lainey roared with laughter.

"I can see today's headlines: *Locals First Date Ends in Stink Bait Caper!*" Della sputtered between giggles.

"Not funny!" Vera sneered. "You're making a mountain out of a mole hill."

"Or compost from tainted stink bait!" Francy laughed and grinned.

It took a couple of minutes for the three ladies to gather their composure. Vera smirked and sipped her coffee, trying not to look at any of them.

"Why do you think Charlie changed his mind?" Lainey asked finally.

Della and Francy looked at Vera.

"Well, it could be that Charlie had some secrets he didn't want known and changed his mind," Vera said sheepishly.

"You were going to expose what he did all those years ago to Shep, weren't you?" Lainey said in amazement.

"That's my Mom," Francy grinned. "Local blackmailer, burglar, getaway car driver, *and* favorite cookie baker!"

CHAPTER 8

The group finished their breakfasts as they talked about the fishing opener and Vera's brush with the law. Once the waitress cleared away their plates, they ordered another pot of coffee.

"Della, I'm eager to know if you found out anything when you looked online," Lainey said. She put her iPad with the printed pages she had inserted on the table.

"It's a bit like looking for a needle in a haystack without the coroner's report," Della began. "Paul thinks they will be able to do DNA testing and hopefully give a name to the body."

"That process can take several weeks depending on the condition, age, and distance to a qualified forensic lab facility," Lainey said. "I was hoping we could get a lead on it before then."

"Did you find anything on the word *gemelos*?" Francy asked.

"What is *gemelos*?" Della asked quickly.

"When Francy and I looked through the pictures last

night, we saw what we think was the name of the boat. *A Gemelos Dream*."

Vera's ears perked up. She leaned forward, resting her elbows on the table. "Gemelos? Is that what you said?"

Lainey looked surprised. "Yes. Do you know that word?"

Vera grinned. "I wasn't born yesterday, you know! I took Spanish in college. It means twin."

Francy looked at Vera. "I never knew you spoke Spanish."

"Before your Dad built his office in town, he filled in at a tiny medical clinic near the South Dakota border. Many of his patients were Hispanic and I was his interpreter."

"I'm impressed, Vera!" Della said smiling. "Paul could use an interpreter at times down at the funeral home."

Vera shook her head. "No way. I can't order off a menu in Spanish anymore. Why I remember gemelos is a mystery."

Lainey grinned. "Well, your memory is spot on." She took out the printed pages and laid them on the table. "It does mean twin or twins."

"A twin's dream," Francy mused. "Why would you name a boat that?"

"Maybe there's a matching boat somewhere? A twin boat?" Della asked.

"Or maybe it's related to the Minnesota Twins baseball team. Maybe a fan named it that," Francy suggested.

"Good question," Lainey answered. "There's a ton of possibilities. I'll ask Sarge when…"

Suddenly, Vera slapped her hand on the table loudly. She looked startled as if someone had scared her.

"What is it Mom? Are you okay?" Francy asked.

Vera blinked a couple of times, then sat back in the booth. "It just dawned on me. Our Mayor was a twin. In fact, his first wife had a miscarriage and they were twins."

Della, Francy, and Lainey looked at each other, wondering what to make of this new information.

"That's good to know," Della began, "but what makes you think that has anything to do with the boat name?"

Vera put her right hand on the table and drummed her fingers slowly. "I'm not saying it does, but I think Mayor Jackson's twin was a bad egg."

"A bad egg? Mom, what do you mean by that?" Francy asked. "He misbehaved or what?"

"I remember something about a young girl that died in a car crash and," Vera paused, "oh, what was the name? Not Melvin, but…"

Francy took a drink of her coffee, then sat it back down before speaking. "We need more to go on than just a girl that might have…"

Vera interrupted her in mid-sentence. "Larry! That's it. Larry Jackson. He was Melvin's twin."

"*Was* his twin?" Lainey asked. "Is he dead? Did he die in the crash, too?"

"I can't remember all the details," Vera answered. "I do recall that Larry seemed to be the one in trouble most of the time. Once, Mrs. Jackson brought Melvin to Doc's office because Larry had pushed him out of their bedroom window.

The window, on the second story, was closed at the time. Poor Melvin was covered with glass shards and wound up with stitches all over his face and arms."

The group fell silent for a couple of minutes and finished their coffees.

"I've got to get going," Lainey said. "I'm going to see if Sarge is at the station."

Della stood up to let Vera out of the booth. "Paul is swamped at work and I told him I'd bring lunch. I'll see if he has heard anything more from the coroner."

"I don't know about Mom, but I'm not used to chauffeuring criminals around in the wee hours of the night. I'm going home to take a nap," Francy grinned.

"You're so funny," Vera said, wrinkling her nose at the remark. "I keep your life interesting… and I am *not* a criminal!"

The group laughed and said their goodbyes. As they walked out of the diner, Lainey noticed a small piece of paper had been put underneath the windshield wiper on her car. She waved to the three ladies and nonchalantly raised the wiper and took the paper. She waited until she was inside the car to read what it said.

Ms. Maynard, I apologize for my rudeness yesterday. It had been a trying day and my attitude toward you was uncalled for. I hope you will forgive me and join me for dinner later this evening. I'm looking forward to getting to know you better. Marv Jackson.

Lainey read the note over a few times, noticing that he left both his cell number and his email address below his name. As she drove to the police station, she kept thinking about their meeting the day before in front of the covered boat.

He had been arrogant, sneaking up behind her, and then trying to intimidate her. He wasn't someone she had expected to hear from or thought twice about. And definitely not someone she'd thought she'd be meeting for a dinner date.

She parked in front of the police station then walked into the entry and pressed the speaker button.

"How can I help you?" the dispatcher's voice asked.

"I'm here to see Sarge. Is he available?"

"He is here. What's your name?"

"I'm Lainey Maynard. I think he was expecting me."

"Wait a moment."

Lainey nodded and looked toward the glass windows where the dispatcher was sitting. It was a new person she had spoken with only a few times. She didn't have to wait long.

"I'll buzz you in. Sarge said to come back to his office."

The door buzzed and Lainey opened it, knowing that she had only a few seconds before it locked again. She said thank you to the dispatcher and made her way down the familiar hallway to Sarge's office. The door was closed and she paused, looking around the hall, before she knocked.

"Come in," Sarge said.

Lainey opened the door slowly. "Is this a bad time? I can come back."

"It's fine. Close the door behind you."

She turned to close the door. Sarge walked out from behind his desk and motioned for her to sit at the small round table in one corner of his office.

"There's coffee in the break room," he said. "Have you had your fix this morning?"

She smiled and chuckled. "I'm okay right now, but I might need more when I leave."

She sat down across from him, took off her coat, and then pulled her iPad out of her backpack.

Sarge leaned back in the chair and waved his hand to stop her from booting up the iPad.

"I don't have any more information. I know you saw the pictures. What questions do you have?"

Lainey could see dark circles around his eyes and guessed that he hadn't had much sleep in the last twenty-four hours. Over the years, she and Sarge had become good friends. They had worked together on many cases and respected each other's talents. She could see how tired he was.

"Thanks for allowing me access to the pictures. I know it will take some time to get the DNA results."

"Forensics will take a couple of weeks. And I know you pretty well. What do you want to ask me?"

Lainey smiled. "Yes, you do know me." She switched on her iPad to take a few notes.

"How many questions are you planning on asking?" Sarge grinned. "Normally, you write a novel of details about every case."

"Only a few," she replied and rolled her eyes. "I like to write things down!"

He nodded. "Go ahead."

"I saw what looked like handcuffs on the steering wheel and on the body. Is that right?"

"Yes."

He's going to give me short answers, which tells me he doesn't have much information. I need to rephrase my questions if I'm going to get anywhere.

"How many bricks did you see that were placed by the body?"

"Trying to get me to answer with more than one word, huh?" Sarge grinned.

She shrugged her shoulders and nodded yes. "Guilty as charged!"

"There were several bricks around the body. I don't have an exact count."

"Did you see any holes in the boat? I mean, did it look like it hit something that would have caused it to sink?"

Sarge hesitated. "It's an active investigation. You know this information is not to be shared with anyone. Not even the Whoopee group."

"You know you can trust me. We've worked together for a long time."

"The boat didn't appear to have any holes in the hull. Nor did it appear that it had been in an accident. Basically, it was intact."

Lainey leaned back in her chair. "It was murder." She had learned to watch Sarge's facial expressions closely. If he was withholding information, his left eye would twitch ever so slightly.

"That has yet to be determined."

"What else could it be?"

Sarge was silent and she saw the slightest of twitches in his eye. She decided to change the subject and do more investigating on her own.

"Have you finished your duties with the fishing opener? Did the Mayor catch any fish?"

"Yes, he caught a few," he leaned forward and crossed his arms. "Good thing Charlie Crowfoot brought fresh bait instead of using Shep and Vera's version." He grinned.

"Oh, yeah," Lainey laughed. "I heard about that! I'm glad he didn't press charges."

He nodded. "Me, too. The last thing I needed was to have Vera behind bars in *my* holding tank. She'd never let me hear the end of it!"

He's smiling. Time to try and get a little more information while he's happy.

"You've been in Mirror Falls for a long time. Do you remember hearing about a local teenaged girl being killed in some sort of car accident? I'm guessing maybe thirty or forty years ago?"

The grin on Sarge's face turned into a straight line, then a frown. He uncrossed his arms, sat up straight in the chair and fixed his gaze on her.

"Why?" he asked flatly.

"No real reason," Lainey began hesitantly, "Vera mentioned something about it at breakfast this morning."

He was silent but kept his eyes focused on her face. Lainey tried not to blink and said nothing.

Finally, Sarge said more forcefully, "WHY?"

Lainey rolled her shoulders and let out a sigh. "I saw the name of the boat was *A Gemelos Dream*. I met for breakfast this morning to see if Della had found information online about any missing boats. Francy came and she made Vera come with her."

Sarge nodded. "And…"

"The word *gemelos* means twin. While we were talking about that, Vera remembered that Mayor Jackson had a twin brother. She thought this twin was a troublemaker and possibly involved in the death of a girl years ago."

She hated to play her hand, but Sarge had left her no choice. She leaned back in her chair, disgusted with herself for giving in.

Sarge rubbed his chin and thought for a moment before responding. "If the Mayor was a twin, that doesn't connect him to the boat." He sighed. "I know you're going to look further into this alleged accident. Promise that you will stay out of trouble. The newspaper has archives. Anyone can search them."

She nodded and grunted, "Okay."

"Wait, I can see by the look on your face, there's something more. What is it?"

Lainey looked at the floor, then looked up at Sarge. "I'll tell you, but don't jump to conclusions."

"You didn't break and enter anywhere, did you?"

"No!" she barked impatiently. "It's nothing illegal. It's something Shep told me."

He let out a big sigh. "What did he say?"

The sarcasm in his voice caused her to change her mind about mentioning the vision. Instead, she answered, "That he doesn't like the green color the Governor painted the walls of his restaurant."

"That's all? He can repaint those walls if he wants to," he smiled. "I've got a lot to do. Call me if you need anything. Otherwise, you'll have to wait until we hear from forensics."

"Thank you, Sarge," she said as she stood up to leave. "I hope you get some rest soon."

"I'm heading home this afternoon. Tell the Whoopees to stay out of trouble."

Lainey smiled and left his office. As she walked down the hallway, she noticed Jarrod, the file clerk, sitting at his desk in the records office.

"Hey, Jarrod," she said walking into the office. "How is your family doing?"

"Hello, Lainey. Good to see you. They're doing fine. Abby is growing like a weed. She's six now and thinks she twenty-six!"

"I'm sure she's not spoiled, either," she grinned. "Have you got a second?"

"Sure. What are you looking for this time?"

"Do you know the last time the evidence room was updated?"

"Updated? What do you mean? The dungeon hasn't been painted in thirty years."

"No," she chuckled. "I don't mean painted updated. I meant how long is evidence stored there? Is it ever destroyed or thrown out because it gets old?"

"Not to my knowledge. The detectives work on cold cases and that evidence could play an important role."

"How old is the oldest piece of evidence in the dungeon?"

"Gosh, I really don't know. You should ask old man Hughes."

"Who? Does he work here?"

Jarrod laughed. "He was the evidence room clerk back in the 60's. He retired about fifteen years ago. He's got to be close to 85 years old by now."

"What is his name? Does he still live in town?"

"Dewayne Hughes. He lives in The Brookshire Senior

Living Center. He used to know every piece of evidence that was stored in the dungeon."

"Thanks! I'll see if he will talk with me. I appreciate your help."

"No problem. See you later."

Lainey smiled and turned to leave. As she walked into the hallway, she waved to the dispatcher and quickly returned to her car. Once inside, she took out her cell phone and called Della. She answered on the first ring.

"Hello, Lainey. How did it go with Sarge?"

"Okay, but not much information. Listen, does Paul happen to know Dewayne Hughes? He retired from the police force fifteen years ago or more."

"Yes, he does. Hold on and I'll get him on the phone."

Lainey waited for just a minute and then Paul was on the phone.

"I know Dewayne. He's a nice man. His room was across the hall from my mother's room when she was there."

"Do you think he would talk to me about his work in the evidence room?"

"I think he'd love to talk about it. He gets lonely. Very few of his friends are still alive. Hold on, I'll get his direct phone number for you."

Paul gave the number and then added, "If you'd like, Della and I can come with you. I haven't seen him in a few years."

"That would be great."

"Tell you what," he began, "I'll call and see when he has time to visit."

"That would be wonderful. Please let me know what he says. I'd really like to ask him a few questions as soon as we could."

"Will do. I'll put Della back on the phone."

"What's this about?" Della asked. "We're going to visit Mr. Hughes? Why?"

"Just a hunch. I've got some work I have to do for the home office. Would you have time to search the internet for birth records? You know, the genealogy site you use?"

"Who am I searching for?"

"Larry Jackson. Birth, death, or marriage. Any information you can find."

"Okay. I'll call if I find anything."

"Great. Talk with you soon."

Lainey ended the call as she drove into her garage. She quickly got out of the car and walked inside her house. She had documents to file for a few cases at work that she had to get completed. She made herself a cup of coffee, using the last of her almond flavored coffee goop. Her cat followed her into her office and jumped up on the computer desk.

"We've got a lot to do, Powie," she said.

CHAPTER 9

Lainey looked at her watch and noticed it was almost 5 o'clock. She had finished the last proposal, emailed it, and then logged off. She walked into the kitchen, saw the note from Marv Jackson sitting beside her backpack, and realized that she had completely forgotten about the odd dinner invitation. She picked up her cell phone and quickly called his number.

Let's see what Marvin Jackson really wants to know.

"Hello, this is Marv."

"Hello, Marvin. This is Lainey Maynard."

His voice softened and was almost dripping with sweetness. "Well, hello to you. I hope you're calling to accept my dinner invitation."

"Do we have enough time to make reservations somewhere? If not, we can reschedule."

"You have a standing reservation with me anytime. I'll pick you up in, say, one hour?"

Lainey looked at her watch, then down at the yoga pants she was wearing and said, "How about we meet at the restaurant instead."

"We're not dining at a restaurant."

"Oh. What are your plans? I need to know how to dress for the occasion."

"I'm sure whatever you wear, you'll look amazing."

"Thank you, Marvin. Just so you know, I always drive my own car when I meet a person for the first dinner date. Where are we going?"

"Spunky little thing, aren't you?"

You, sir, have no idea.

"No, just being practical."

He laughed loudly. "You win… this time. I'll be at the marina on Ness Lake in an hour."

Before she could say anything else, Marvin ended the call. She thought for a moment, then called Francy. She wanted to make sure someone knew where she was going and who she was with.

"He wants to meet you at the old marina for dinner?" Francy asked in disbelief. "That makes no sense. What do you think he's up to?"

"I'm not sure," Lainey replied. "That's why I'm letting you know to keep your phone handy. If I need something, I'll call."

"Want me to call the station and have an officer drive by a couple of times?"

"No, I think it will be fine. Thanks, though."

"Call me when you get home and give me the details."

"You got it. By the way, is Vera at home tonight or does she have another date with Shep?"

Francy laughed. "I told her she's grounded. I need to get a good night's sleep!"

"They make a cute couple… kinda like Bonnie and Clyde!"

They both giggled. "I'll tell Mom you said that. Talk to you later."

Lainey hung up and put her phone on its charger while she showered. She wanted to make sure her battery was at 100% before meeting with Marvin Jackson. By 5:45, she was in her car and driving toward Ness Lake.

There were several cars parked around the marina and she wasn't sure which one belonged to Marvin. She pulled into an empty space, took out her cell phone, and called his number.

"Don't tell me you're standing me up!" he said when he answered the phone.

"No, I didn't know if you were here. You failed to tell me what car you were driving."

"Do you see the large houseboat docked on the left of the marina?"

Lainey glanced around and found two boats parked next to each other. "I see two houseboats."

"Do you see the one that has the University of Minnesota flag flying on top? The name of the boat is *Ultimo Ganador*. I'll be waiting on deck to help you aboard."

"All right. See you in a minute."

She ended the call and put her cell phone in her jacket pocket. She got out of the car and began walking to the houseboat. As she got closer, she saw Marvin standing on the front deck of the boat, waving at her. She walked down the ramp to where the boat was anchored. He met her and offered his hand to help her step up into the boat.

"Thank you," Lainey said after she was safely on the boat.

"The light shimmering off the water makes you look even lovelier," he answered, grinning like a Cheshire cat that just ate a canary. He held on to her hand longer than she wanted him to.

He has something up his sleeve. I've got to keep my guard up.

"This is a beautiful boat. Is it yours?" she said, pulling her hand away from his grip.

"It belongs to my Dad. But I use it whenever I want to. Let's go inside. Dinner is waiting."

Marvin opened the main cabin door and the aroma of freshly baked bread filled the air. Lainey walked into a lavishly decorated living room complete with leather couches, recliners, and end tables. The curtains on each of the windows were gold and maroon. The entire room was covered with Minnesota Gopher football memorabilia including trophies and many action pictures of Marvin's football days.

"This is quite the collection of your time as a Gopher," Lainey said, trying to break the awkward silence.

"Dad collected all of my awards," Marvin spouted proudly, touching, and admiring one of the trophies. "These are just a few that would fit in the room. I believe our dinner is waiting. Please, follow me."

She followed as he walked down a narrow hallway at the back of the living room. Her eyes opened wide when she saw a table set for two with a maroon tablecloth, glistening white dishes with gold trimming, and two tall candles lit in the middle. A beautiful young woman pulled out a cloth-covered chair and motioned for her to sit down.

"Thank you," Lainey said.

"You're welcome," the woman replied. She walked over and pulled out the chair for Marvin as well. He nodded to her and she returned to the galley kitchen.

"I didn't realize you have staff on this boat," Lainey commented.

"Cheri caters dinners for Dad and me when we have special guests. I think you'll love her Broiled Dijon Walleye. Some say it's to die for."

That's an interesting choice of words, Marv. Let's see why you brought me here.

"I am surprised that you asked me tonight," she said calmly.

Cheri brought out wine, poured a little in each of their glasses, then sat the bottle in an ice bucket next to Marvin.

"I hope you like Chardonnay," he said, taking a sip. "It pairs nicely with our main course."

Lainey nodded. She wasn't a big fan of wine but took a sip to be polite.

He finished his glass and took the wine bottle to pour himself more. "We didn't meet under the best of circumstances the other day and after I thought about it, I wanted to start over again."

"If I remember correctly, you called me a nosey investigator," she said flatly, staring directly into his eyes.

He grinned and nodded. "Yes, I did. And yes... you are."

She was silent but kept studying his face.

He took another large drink of his wine and said, "Some would take that as a compliment."

Again, she didn't answer. Cheri had brought their dinner and was serving a large portion of the walleye on her plate.

"That's plenty, thank you," Lainey said, stopping Cheri from heaping more on her plate. She politely waited for Marvin to be served and then took a bite. The strong and spicy Dijon mustard caused her to immediately begin coughing. She grabbed her water glass to wash down the bite and cool her throat.

He laughed as he watched her. "We like things hot around here. It's part of my heritage."

Her eyes began to water and when she had caught her breath, she patted them dry with her napkin.

"I apologize. That first bite took me by surprise."

"We've always loved our food spicy," he said. "I can remember when my grandmother used to make homemade salsa. It was three times as hot as this."

"You mentioned your heritage. What is your background?"

"My grandfather was born in Minnesota, but my grandmother was born in Brazil. My dad, mother, and I are proud to be born and raised in Minnesota."

Lainey nodded. "You didn't answer when I asked why you called me for a dinner date."

Marvin put down his fork and leaned forward in his chair, putting his elbows on the table. He folded his hands together and said, "I think we need to get to know one another."

"I've lived in Mirror Falls for many years and we haven't met before. Why now?"

He studied her for a moment, moving his gaze from her eyes to her chest and back to her eyes. She knew he was trying to make her feel uncomfortable. She didn't flinch and kept her focus on his face.

"I keep busy with appearances, promotions, and fundraisers for the Gophers athletics department. I have an apartment in the Cities and don't get to Mirror Falls very often. I guess we've never had the opportunity to meet." He paused, picked up his wine glass, and drank the remainder quickly. He poured the rest of the wine from the bottle into his glass and motioned for Cheri to bring another bottle.

"Marvin, let's…"

"Call me Marv," he interrupted. She could see that he was beginning to feel no pain from the wine and didn't want to wait until he had polished off another bottle.

"Marvin, let's cut to the chase. When we met the other day, it was obvious that we did not have a romantic connection of any kind. There is a reason I'm here. What is it?"

He deliberately gulped down his fourth glass of wine and poured another from the second bottle.

"When a dead body shows up during the fishing opener in my Dad's town, I get involved. And it's an election year."

She hesitated a moment, looking to see if Cheri was standing close by. She wasn't. She put her hand in her pocket and felt her cell phone.

"How would this affect his re-election bid?"

"Even you know it's not the best type of publicity. He's talked to the police and wants to wrap up the investigation quickly and quietly." He took a few more gulps from his wine glass. "I'm helping him tie up loose ends."

Lainey nodded and cautiously asked, "He thinks I'm a loose end?"

He shrugged his shoulders, sat back in his chair, and put one arm over the back of it. "Dad prefers only law enforcement officials work on this case."

"I see. So this dinner date was to let me know to stop nosing around," she stated.

"You're not as dense as some say you are," he laughed and emptied his glass once more.

The hair on the back of her neck bristled at his remark. She got up quickly, pushing in her chair.

"I'll see myself out," she said, trying not to show her anger.

"Don't fall off the boat. I understand it's hard to float in cold water."

She walked briskly back through the hallway and the living room and stepped onto the boat ramp. As an afterthought, she took out her phone and took a picture of the houseboat. She walked to her car, glancing to make sure no one was following her. She got inside, locked the door, and headed home.

Once she was safely inside her house, she pulled out her iPad to make notes about her so-called date with Marvin Jackson. She wanted to make sure she wrote down the details while they were fresh in her mind. She was still angry at his insulting remarks and his conceited personality.

She had a routine of listing questions at the bottom of her notes. Why did the Mayor think she was a loose end? And did he think she would be enamored with his celebrity son? The election was months away. Did the Mayor really think publicity about this could hurt his chances of winning? Or was that another lie Marvin had told her.

She saved the notes and opened her Outlook email. She glanced quickly at any that might be urgent. There was one email subject line that caught her eye. It was from Francy and said only three words: suicide or murder?

Lainey opened the email and began reading. The initial investigation report suspected someone had committed suicide, but that a final decision was pending waiting on identification and DNA testing.

She picked up her cell and called Francy, who picked up after a couple of rings.

"How was your big dinner date? Any second dates?"

"Mayor Jackson thinks I'm a loose end and sent good old Marv to deal with me," she said disgustedly.

"What? What in the world happened?"

"Long story, but he drank almost two bottles of wine by himself. The tipsier he became, the more his true repulsive nature came out. The entire dinner was a charade geared toward intimidating me to stop investigating the murder. He's a conceited jerk."

"I've heard others say that about our local football hero. Did you see my message? First reports are that the person in the boat committed suicide."

"Have you spoken with Sarge? What are his thoughts?"

"I haven't had a chance to talk with him, but I'm questioning how you can sink a boat and handcuff yourself to the steering wheel. Isn't that going to a lot of trouble?"

"That's a good question. I'm coming to the station in the morning and talk with Sarge. By the way, I wonder if Della has found any old articles about missing persons? Have you spoken with her?"

"I haven't thought about it, sorry. Shep asked Mom and me to his place for supper."

Lainey laughed loudly. "Wait...now you're a chaperone? For your mom and her boyfriend?"

Francy chuckled. "He felt bad about getting arrested the other night and wanted to make it up to me. He made the best chicken tetrazzini I've ever eaten!"

"He's probably sincere and I know he's a terrific cook."

"It was a bit awkward when Mom suggested Charlie come too."

Lainey gasped. "You're kidding. Vera, Shep, *and* Charlie having dinner in the same room? I can't believe it!"

"It was strange, but we ate and made small talk. Let's say everyone was trying hard to be cordial."

"Wonders never cease."

"You got that right. I'll meet you tomorrow at the station. What time are you planning on going?"

Lainey looked at her work calendar and found a time that she had open. "I'm thinking around 11. Hopefully Sarge will be available then."

"Sounds good. You might shoot him an email tonight. If he's busy, he'll let you know."

"Will do. Talk to you tomorrow."

They said goodbye and ended the call. She sent a short email to Sarge and then got ready for bed.

Della had scoured through newspaper archives until the early hours of the morning trying to find any articles of car accidents, dead teenagers, or Larry Jackson. She sat back in her chair, rubbing her eyes, and was going to call it a night when she suddenly heard the familiar ping notification sound of a new email in her inbox. She quickly opened Outlook and saw a new email from the Mirror Falls Historical Society Museum.

Earlier that evening, Della had sent an email asking if they had any articles saved from decades old newspapers. The response email confirmed that they did have access to old microfiche files and newspapers that dated back more than one hundred years and that she was welcome to come by and view them during regular business hours.

Excited to have at least one lead from her hours of searching, Della set her alarm clock for 7:00 a.m. She emailed Lainey and Francy to meet her promptly at 8:00 a.m., the time the museum office opened. She powered down her computer, yawned, and headed to catch a few hours of sleep.

"The girls will be surprised to see me bright-eyed and bushy-tailed that early in the morning," she whispered to a half-asleep Paul.

"Yeah, sure, bushy-tailed," he mumbled sleepily.

CHAPTER 10

Francy and Lainey were eager to get access to the files Della's email had promised but surprised at the early morning appointment time. Both ladies were standing beside their cars in front of the historical society building by 7:45 a.m.

"I didn't think Della could function this early in the morning," Francy chuckled.

Lainey grinned and held up a silver Yeti cup. "I brought a hot toasted butter pecan cream for her just in case she hasn't had her cup of java."

"How long do you think we'll need to wait..." Francy stopped in mid-sentence as she saw Della pulling into the parking lot. "Well, what do you know? She's actually early!"

Della parked her car next to Lainey's, got out waving her hand to greet them.

"Bet you thought I'd be late, didn't you?" she teased.

Francy glanced at Lainey, then back at Della. "Now why would we think that?"

Lainey smiled. "You must have a loud alarm clock, my

friend. I've called you before in the early morning and couldn't get an answer."

"It's like trying to wake the dead," Francy added.

Della's eyes twinkled a little and she grinned. "Well, Paul can be a persuasive alarm clock."

Francy rolled her eyes and whined. "Geesh…we don't need the details."

"I brought you coffee just in case," Lainey laughed as she handed the Yeti to Della. "What do you think we'll find in here?"

Della grabbed the cup of coffee, took a big sip, and said, "Ah…you know my favorite. Thank you!"

As they walked toward the entrance of the building, Della told them she had emailed Agnes Mitchell, the historian and curator of the local museum, to see if there were any files, newspapers, or information on missing persons or mysterious deaths over the last twenty or thirty years. Agnes had responded that the museum did indeed have old microfiche that had recently been copied over to DVD and that she was welcome to search to her heart's content.

"Agnes said to come during business hours only," Della finished. "And they are open from 8 till noon. I thought we better get crackin' early."

Lainey nodded. "Were you able to find any birth records for Mayor Jackson or a Larry Jackson?"

"It's a bit odd, but I found only one record for Larry Jackson, and it was an old court indictment," Della replied.

They heard footsteps coming toward the front door, then a couple of clicks, and the massive double doors were pulled open. The outside of the building looked like a century old brick house with three stories. Each corner had a round column with a bay window and pointed decorative trim that extended upward on each of the three stories. Each rounded corner had a pointed, gabled roof with lattice trim that resembled wooden lace. The spire on each of the four points was adorned with a wrought iron weathervane arrow twirling above a cross with the four directions on it.

The once bright white pillars that proudly held up the large porch were now faded, cracked, and scarred from the strain of a hundred harsh Minnesota winters. The grand double front door of the mansion still welcomed strangers with its ornate stained glass that covered the entire length of the door panels. The intricate paisley-like patterns of reds, greens, blues, and oranges, created images of starbursts that seemed as vibrant as the day they were inlaid. The glass glistened when the early morning sunshine hit it.

"Welcome to the Mirror Falls Historical Society Museum," a small, charming, older lady said as she motioned for them to come inside. "I'm Agnes Mitchell. Please, come in."

The three ladies walked inside and were instantly transported back to the early 1900's. They stood in amazement, gazing at the enormous grand entry hall's dark cherry woodwork, and the regal staircase. The smell of musty pine was heavy in the air. The tall walls were covered with a collage of old paintings, each unique in its size, shape, and subject. Each encased in a larger than life gold or silver elaborately decorated frame. Their host's voice brought them back to reality.

"It's breathtaking the first time you visit, isn't it?" Agnes sighed sweetly. "I've always loved this house."

"I remember visiting this place years ago on a grade school field trip," Francy began, "but I'd forgotten how beautiful it is."

Agnes nodded. "Many people have visited the Glensheen Mansion in Duluth, the James J. Hill House in St. Paul, and the Turnblad Mansion in Minneapolis. But lovely homes like ours, tucked away in small rural and farming areas sometimes can be forgotten."

"Mrs. Mitchell, I'm Della Kristiansen, the person who

emailed you about looking through your newspaper archives."

"It's a pleasure to meet you. Please, call me Aggie. And your friends are?"

"This is Francy Baines and Lainey Maynard."

"Well, hello to all of you. I'm so happy to share our little bit of history with you. How may I help you?"

"We'd like to look through the archives about a car accident that killed a local teen some years ago," Della answered.

"We'll have to go downstairs to the basement. Please be careful," Agnes cautioned, "we haven't had the funds to repair or update that area. It's dark and moldy, but the information you are looking for should be stored there."

She walked ahead of the group. "The only safe entrance to the basement is through the kitchen. Follow me."

"Is there another way to get into the basement?" Lainey asked as she followed in line behind Agnes, Della and Francy.

"There was a cellar door in the floor of the detached parking garage that led down to the basement, but the wooden stairs have rotted and that entrance was condemned by the city years ago. I can't remember the last time it might have been used."

As the group walked quietly through the winding hallway, past bedrooms and old bathrooms, Agnes talked briefly, highlighting the historical importance of each room, as if she were guiding another tour. The ladies smiled politely, listening and looking, but anxiously waiting to get to work searching the old files.

Finally, they walked into an old, green-tiled kitchen. The tall, white-washed cabinets with their tarnished handles and knobs seemed to straighten themselves just a little in hopes someone would touch or open them once more.

"This was the servants' kitchen. Very modest, but still modern for the day," Agnes said as she walked toward a door at the end of the room. "The door to the basement is inside the pantry."

She opened the pantry door and flipped on the light switch. The small room had faded paint spots and holes in the walls showing where old shelves must have been anchored at one time. At the end of the room was a door that couldn't have been more than four feet tall.

"We do have some lights, but there are no windows. Please watch your step as you descend." Agnes opened the tiny door, ran her hand over the right side of the wall and turned on the light.

"You ladies go first. I will follow to make sure you are okay."

Lainey nodded and bent down to avoid hitting her head on the door. A stone stairway curved downward and there was no handrail. She put her right hand on the wall to steady herself and unexpectedly was startled at the slimy wetness she felt.

"Yuck. Be careful, everyone," she said as she wiped her hand on her pant leg. "The walls are grimy and wet from moisture."

Della cringed but followed Lainey. Francy touched the wall with her first two fingers, then rubbed them with her thumb. She raised her hand and sniffed, trying to identify the odd smell and texture.

"This stuff is like rust," Francy said as she walked down the stairs, "why would the walls have rust residue on them?"

A large room at the bottom of the stairs was cold and the air smelled of mold and mildew. The dirt floor was rock hard and there were no windows. The wooden beams on the ceiling were laced to the stone walls with thick, grey cobwebs acting as a hanging graveyard for spiders and bugs. Wooden sawhorses with particle boards for tops were lined up against one side of the room. Each held several boxes and trash bags piled several feet high. A couple of two drawer metal filing cabinets set underneath each of the make-shift tables. A thick layer of dust covered everything.

"As I mentioned, we haven't had the funds to do the necessary care to preserve these documents," Aggie said sadly. "Such important history of our town and it's rotting away."

Della agreed. "Aggie, would you happen to know where we should look? The accident could have been forty years ago or more."

Francy and Lainey were listening while walking around the room looking for anything that might help them.

"Hey, Lainey," Francy whispered, motioning to the other end of the room. "This must be the door to the stairway from the garage entrance."

"It's like a metal cellar door. Let's see if it's locked."

Lainey glanced back at Della and Aggie, then gently tried to open the door. It moved a little. She pulled harder and the door made a loud creaking sound before opening slightly. Everyone in the room heard the door, so she pulled harder and it opened about a foot.

"That is the door to the outside," Aggie stated, shaking her head. "I told you the stairway was condemned and closed off."

Lainey wasn't sure if Aggie was angered or amused or simply confused. Francy was trying not to smile.

"I wanted to see if any files might have been left in there."

Francy rolled her eyes as if to say how lame that answer sounded as Aggie and Della walked over to them.

In a quiet voice, Aggie smiled and looked into the face of each of them, one at a time. Then she took a deep breath in and sighed.

"I've lived here all my life. My family has lived here for generations. And I've witnessed everything from the invention of television, wars, presidential assassinations, and man landing on the moon. You girls are looking for information on Beverly Daschel's death, aren't you? Why?"

Her abruptness stunned the three friends for a second as they looked at each other. Finally, Lainey spoke up first.

"Yes, Ma'am. I think we are, but we didn't have the name of the young girl."

Francy nodded. "A body was found a few days ago and we're trying to figure out who it might be and if it is connected to the accident."

Aggie closed her eyes and replied, "I knew someone would eventually find him. Poor soul."

"What? Who? Please tell us what you know," Della said. "Is the information in the files down here? I thought you said the information had been transferred to DVD's?"

"Part of it has been," Aggie replied. "A few newspapers and items were missed. And part of our historical information was destroyed in a fire years ago." She walked over to one stack of boxes and then bent down to the small filling cabinet below it. She carefully pulled open the bottom drawer. "I think the information you want may be in this file. Please take what you need and let's go upstairs to talk."

The drawer contained newspapers, some wrapped in plastic and some in leather envelope binders. There was also a small box labeled *Photos*. Francy grabbed all of the newspapers and binders, then handed Lainey the box. They quickly made their way back to the main floor.

Once in the kitchen, Aggie led them upstairs to the office area she used. The small room was decorated with flowered wallpaper, flowered curtains, and a small love seat that faced the bay window. Toward the middle of the room was a round table covered with a paisley tablecloth. An antique blue glass vase of fresh carnations sat in the middle with a set of eyeglasses next to them.

"Here is where I come to work and think," Aggie said, smiling. "Back in the day, this was known as the parlor. Guests would be served tea and cookies to end their visit. Let's see what you found and perhaps I can answer your questions."

The ladies put their dusty parcels on the table and sat down. Aggie put on the reading glasses and unwrapped the first stack of newspapers. She glanced through the first couple of pages. Then she laid them on the table and looked at the ladies.

"The Jackson family have been hard workers since I can remember. Edward and Josephine, the grandparents of Melvin, were farmers that worked as hard as anyone to put food on their table. He and his wife did have a set of twins, but one died within a few days of his birth. Poor Josephine thought it was her fault and never forgave herself. They pampered the surviving twin, Marty, and gave him everything they possibly could."

Aggie stopped and sighed. She rubbed her eyes to wipe away little tears that were forming. She smiled, looked down, and then back up at them.

"Marty did pretty well, but there was little money for him to go to college. He had big aspirations, though, and became an apprentice at the newspaper. He enjoyed the spotlight of being the only reporter in town and very quickly let the attention go to his head. He married a sweet girl, Liza Martinez, whose well-to-do family had moved from Mexico to start a new life. Her father was running for mayor at the time."

"I see," Francy grinned. "He married her to get into politics, correct?"

"That's what the town thought. But Liza was crazy about him. She and I were best friends all through school. Once she became Mrs. Martin Jackson, she didn't spend much time with me." A sadness came over Aggie's face.

"Marty only allowed her to socialize with prominent citizens. My family were dairy farmers. I wore hand-me-down clothes and worked in the dairy while she shopped in the Twin Cities and had her hair done."

"You seem to have been good friends," Della said trying to comfort her. "I'm sure Liza valued your friendship."

"I like to think so," Aggie smiled.

"Did Martin and Liza have twin boys? Melvin and Larry?" Lainey asked. "I heard that Larry might have been in trouble at some point?"

"Sadly, Larry was a troublemaker. Even when they were youngsters, Melvin was kind, funny, helpful. Larry seemed angry all the time and jealous of any attention Melvin got. Liza prayed over that boy until her dying day."

"What happened to Larry? Is he connected to Beverly Daschel's death?" Francy questioned.

"Beverly was a high school cheerleader. Sweet and popular. She fell head over heels for Larry even though her parents didn't approve. One night, she told them she was going to the movies with her girlfriends, and instead went with Larry in his car."

"Larry was driving when the accident happened?" Della asked.

Aggie nodded, reaching for another set of newspapers. She was quiet as she looked through several of them. Then suddenly she stopped, put one on the table and said, "Yes. The accident made the front page of the newspaper."

"Accident Takes Life of Mirror Falls Teen" was the headline. A large picture of a mangled car wrapped around a tree trunk was directly underneath. The article said Larry Jackson, age 17, was driving and lost control of his car. His passenger, Beverly Daschel, age 16, died instantly in the

crash. Services were pending. And that was all the information listed.

"This was the only article that appeared in the Mirror Falls paper about the accident. I'm sure it was because Martin was running the newspaper and didn't want Larry's name involved," Aggie stated.

"There must have been an investigation," Francy began. "What caused Larry to lose control?"

Aggie put both hands on the table and her voice became a little harsher. "Martin tried hard to keep this out of the limelight but couldn't. You see, Larry left the scene... and Beverly. He had been drinking and only suffered bruises. When he saw that she was dead, he got scared and ran away. The police quickly found out and Larry was arrested for drinking and driving." She paused, frowned, and then shook her head.

"What did Martin do?" Lainey asked. "He must have been devastated."

"Yes. Martin did his best to talk or perhaps buy Larry's freedom. But a young girl had been killed. The boy was indicted, and a trial was scheduled in the Twin Cities Criminal Court."

Della had been listening and looking through more papers. She found a small court records section, folded it over, and put in on the table, pointing to the words.

"It says that Larry disappeared before the trial could begin. Do you think Martin helped him escape?"

Lainey and Francy looked at each other, both thinking the same thing.

They think Larry committed suicide to escape the trial.

"Yes, I do. Martin swore that Larry was in his room when he went to bed and gone by the next morning," Aggie replied.

A light bulb went off in Lainey's head and she was suddenly covered in goose bumps.

"Aggie, did the Jackson's happen to own a boat?" she questioned.

The older lady smiled and pointed her finger toward Lainey. "You've done your homework, I see. Yes, the Jackson's boat was pristine, shiny and fast. Fancy, just like Martin wanted. Even the name stood out in our little town. When Larry disappeared, the boat was never seen again."

"And the name of the boat..." Lainey leaned forward and asked excitedly, "do you happen to remember the name of the boat?"

"Sure do. It was called *A Gemelos Dream.*"

CHAPTER 11

L ainey's heart skipped a beat when Aggie mention *A Gemelos Dream*. She glanced at Della and Francy to see if they had the same reaction. She took a moment to gather her composure and try to control her excitement before she spoke.

"Aggie, you are positive that was the name?"

"Marty stored that boat in one of our barns during the winter months. Every year before he came to get it, I had to clean and scrub it. He wanted it spotless. I will never forget the name of that boat."

Lainey sat back in her chair, rubbing her forehead in thought.

If Larry committed suicide in the boat, how did he do that? There were no holes in the hull.

Francy was watching Lainey and as if reading her mind said, "We need to look at the boat pictures more closely. I didn't see any holes, did you?"

Aggie had been sitting quietly, observing the three ladies. "The boat they pulled out of the lake recently was the *Gemelos Dream*, wasn't it?"

Della nodded. "Yes, it was. And there was a body inside the boat."

Aggie sadly shook her head. "I'm glad Liza isn't alive to relive this tragedy. She suffered so when Larry went missing."

For a moment, the room was eerily silent as if it were in mourning. Aggie let out a loud sigh, breaking the spell of the quietness.

"Melvin took Larry's disappearance very hard," she began. "Marty said it was as if he took on some of his brother's bad habits."

"What kind of bad habits?" Francy questioned, leaning forward, and putting her elbows on the table.

"The public believed Larry had taken the boat and vanished. Rumors of what might have happened, where he might be hiding, brought more pain to Liza. When Melvin was burned in the fire only a few weeks after Larry disappeared, she wouldn't leave her bedroom or speak to anyone. She died a few months later. I think it was from a broken heart."

Lainey's mind was racing. "Fire? Melvin was burned in what fire?"

"The fire that destroyed more than half of our historical records. You see, at the time, these were stored in a large metal shed on the Jackson's property."

Aggie flipped through more newspapers and added, "I'm sure the story is in one of these pages."

Della frowned as she ruffled through pages of newspapers. "Did anyone think Larry would have killed himself?"

"No. Most people knew him as a coward, a boaster, a bully. Some thought he drove the boat into a remote lake location and scuttled it to make it look like an accident. Then disappeared in Canada."

"Wonder why the police didn't drag any of the lakes

around town?" Della questioned. "Isn't that usually what they do when a boat goes missing?"

Aggie smiled. "My dear, we have many, many lakes in this county alone. Unless someone reported seeing the boat or pieces of the boat, they wouldn't have known where to start looking."

"You said Melvin began behaving badly," Lainey said, hoping to get the answer to Francy's earlier question. "What did you mean?"

"Melvin had always been polite, quiet, even outgoing. But after Larry disappeared, it was like he became a double personality. He'd be ever so nice, helping carry groceries, mowing people's lawns... and then suddenly become angry, bitter, and... mean."

Della looked around the table. "Mean? Did he hurt anyone?"

Aggie shrugged. "Maybe rude is a better word. I remember being in the post office, standing in line to buy postage stamps. Melvin was two or three people in front of me. The worker behind the counter was telling him they did not have the package that he was expecting."

She paused and shuddered. "He started yelling at the poor man. He reached over the counter and grabbed him by the shirt, demanding he go to the back and look for his package. When the worker left to go to the backroom, Melvin turned to those of us in the line and with a cold, deep, growling voice *ordered* everyone to stop staring and mind their own business. I thought he was going to hurt someone."

Francy and Lainey exchanged glances, each one nodding.

"I'm sure that was disturbing, especially when he didn't usually behave like that. Thank you for sharing with us," Della said. She stood up and walked over to give Aggie a hug.

"We've taken up too much of your time," Lainey said. "We

need to be going. Would you mind if we take these things with us? We promise to bring them back safe and sound."

"Of course," Aggie smiled. "I don't get many visitors these days and it's been wonderful to have someone in the parlor again. Makes me feel like a young girl."

The group gathered up the papers and box of photos and followed Aggie downstairs. She opened the grand doors and waved to them as they walked down the steps.

"If there is anything further I can help you with, please don't be strangers. You're always welcome!"

The three waved to say goodbye and Lainey spoke as soon as they were standing far enough away that Aggie couldn't hear.

"Girls, let's go to my house. Della, you can use my computer to look up details about this fire while Francy and I go through the photos and newspapers with a fine-tooth comb."

"Don't you have a meeting with Sarge around 11?" Francy asked.

"I don't want to talk with him until we have more information. I'll call and cancel on the way to my house. See you there in a few minutes."

They each got into their cars and followed Lainey to her house. Once inside, they laid out all of the bundles on the kitchen table and sat down to start digging in.

"I need coffee," Della stated. "Where's your Keurig? I'll make us each a cup."

"It's in the pantry on the bottom shelf. Coffee pods are next to it," Lainey answered. "I've got some chocolate chip oatmeal cookies in a bag in the drawer below."

"Can we bring your laptop in here so Della can search while we look through these papers?" Francy asked.

"You bet," Lainey replied. "It'll take just a minute to get setup."

By the time Della had the coffee and cookies ready, Lainey had her laptop up and running. Francy was flipping through various newspaper articles they had previously seen.

"I'm very interested in the fire Aggie told us about," Francy said. "Seems odd that I don't remember hearing about it. Wonder if Mom does?" She pulled out her cell phone and called Vera.

"Hello, sweetie," Vera answered. "Are you filling in at the station today?"

"Hi, Mom. No, I'm at Lainey's with Della. Do you remember a fire over at the old Jackson place years ago?"

Vera didn't answer for several moments. "The three of you are snooping around without me?"

"Well," Francy started to explain, but was abruptly interrupted.

"Don't bother. I know when I'm not wanted. Seems you only include this poor, old, withered woman when you're stumped on something ancient from the past," Vera said slowly, trying hard to make her voice crack.

Della and Lainey giggled, putting their hands over their mouths to keep from laughing.

"Mom, that was pathetic! Yes, come over, we need you."

"Good. I'll bring banana nut bread."

"Fine. See you in a few minutes." Francy rolled her eyes as she ended the call. She looked at the other two and laughed. "Only Mom would think we'd buy that sappy story!"

"At least we're getting banana nut bread," Della squeaked out between chuckles.

It wasn't long before Vera was sitting at the table and Francy was telling her what they had found.

"This is the information Aggie let us take from the basement of the museum. I called to see if you remembered the fire."

"Agnes is an amazing person. She has been the only

person in this town that has tried to keep the museum going. Bless her soul," Vera smiled. "I've known her for years."

Lainey had opened the box of photos and was looking through them, listening to the conversation. Della was busy searching the internet for any records of the fire, or Larry, and not really paying much attention to anyone else. Vera and Francy were going through the newspapers, trying to find something.

"I do remember it," Vera said as she folded a page in half and pointed to a picture at the top. "See, this is a picture of the barn after the fire."

Francy took the paper and started reading aloud.

"Last week's fire at the Jackson's farm destroyed more than the family's barn and equipment. Martin Jackson, president of the historical society, said the museum was using his barn to store their historical documents, pictures, furniture, and other items while their building was being renovated. Of the dozens of boxes of irreplaceable memories, only a few were salvaged. Jackson's son, Melvin, was released from the hospital today after suffering burns to his hands while fighting the fire. He is expected to have a full recovery."

"Does the article say what caused the fire?" Francy asked.

"No. Maybe it's in an earlier article?" Della replied.

"I'll check that out at the police station. There should be reports in the dungeon."

Lainey put the pictures down and looked at Vera. "Did you tell us Doc treated Melvin?"

"He stitched Melvin up after Larry shoved him out a second story bedroom window. Poor boy had cuts all over his face and arms. But when the fire happened, Martin had his boy airlifted to the Twin Cities to a specialized burn unit."

"It's the first time I've heard about Melvin being burned," Francy said. "Guess he healed up nicely."

Vera sighed. "The car accident, Larry's disappearance, and the barn fire happened within weeks of each other. Marvin kept the news media away from Melvin... and once Liza died, he made sure the fire was forgotten."

Della blinked and rubbed her eyes. "That's a lot of tragedy for any family to deal with in such a short period of time."

"Martin Jackson knew better than anyone how to manipulate the media."

"And how to bury any information he didn't want people to remember." Francy mused.

"That's true," Lainey replied as she laid two photos on the table, "but maybe pictures *can* say a thousand words. These are a little bit faded, but if you look at the one on the left, it's clearly the Jackson twins."

Vera picked up the photo first. "Yes, it is. Goodness, they do look identical." She handed the photo to Francy, who passed it on to Della.

"Are they standing on the old football field?" Francy asked.

"I believe so. They must have been around sixteen or seventeen?" Vera answered.

"Why would the museum have a picture of them standing on the field? How is that historical?" Della asked, putting the photo down on the table.

Lainey smiled. "Look closely at what's behind them."

Vera slapped the table. "My gosh, that was the year Martin donated a new football scoreboard to the school. They are standing in front of it!"

"Yep. Looks like Martin wanted to make sure his boys were included in the history."

"What's in the second photo?" Della asked.

"It's a little more recent," Lainey said, passing the photo around the table, giving each one a moment to look it over. "You tell me."

Vera picked up the photo and put it down several times before she spoke. "It's Hill Annex Mine."

Lainey nodded.

"That's a state park now," Francy commented, picking the photo up to take a closer look.

"Della, type in Hill Annex Mine and see what Google has to say about it," Lainey said.

"Gotta love Google," Della remarked. "It says it's an abandoned iron open-pit mine that has been turned into a tourist center."

She read aloud that the mine, once the sixth largest in Minnesota, is located in the Mesabi Range of northern Minnesota. It produced some 63 million tons of iron ore before it closed in 1978. When it closed, the pumps that had been used to keep water out of the mine were shut down. The water flooded the open pit creating a large man-made lake. Over the years, conservationists added vegetation to encourage black bear, deer, coyote, and raptors like eagles and hawks. It was declared a state park in the late 80's.

"Why was Melvin Jackson visiting the park when this photo was taken? Another photo opportunity for him?" Francy asked.

Della picked up the photo again. "This must have been an event or something. He's standing with several others, including his son, Marvin. He's still in college because he's wearing his Gopher dress football jersey."

"I'm guessing they were presenting something to the park director," Lainey replied. "The reason I held this photo out is because of who is standing *behind* them."

Della peered into the photo then gasped. "I didn't even notice that!" She handed the photo to Francy and Vera who each examined the photo again.

"Is that... nah, it can't be," Francy said in surprise. "He looks so young!"

Vera scratched her head. "You got me. Who are you referring to?"

"It's Quincy Yelnick," Della replied disgustedly. "The guy who tried to cause trouble the night before the fishing opener. He may have more hair in this photo, but I won't forget his face."

"Can you enlarge these pictures?" Francy asked Lainey.

"I'll try. Sometimes old photos get grainy and blurry when I enlarge them with my copier."

"If that doesn't work, Paul has a nice photo scanning machine that he uses many times on old photos families bring him. They come out fairly clear," Della added.

"Would you ask him to do it? I'd really like to see these close up as soon as possible," Lainey asked.

Francy caught a glimpse of a familiar twinkle in Lainey's eyes as she handed the photos to Della.

"Okay, my friend. Fess up. What's really going on in that brain of yours? What's bothering you?"

Lainey grinned.

"Well, tell us!" Vera encouraged.

"I'm extremely curious to know *how* and *why* the photo at the mine got inside this box. It was taken years after the fire... and supposedly, years after anyone had access to the basement of the museum."

CHAPTER 12

Della returned her attention to the computer screen and was typing away while the others continued to look through papers.

"I'm sure there is a connection, but where is it?" Francy muttered, shaking her head. "My fingers are black from the old newspaper print."

Lainey had been studying the photo at the mine. She put it on the table and looked at Della. "I wonder if we can search for any business ventures or companies that Melvin and Quincy might be involved in?"

Della looked up and smiled. "I'm two steps ahead of you! It's going to take some time, though."

"I know. Do you think Paul can blow these pictures up this afternoon?"

"I think so. I'll bring him some of Vera's banana nut bread with the photos. He's rather good about conforming when food is involved!"

The ladies giggled.

Vera had an impish grin on her face and a tiny sparkle in

her eyes. "I might have someone who could shed some light on any history between Yelnick and Jackson."

"That would be terrific! Who?" Lainey asked excitedly.

Francy's mouth curved upward in a crooked, half smile. "It's Shep. Right, Mom?"

Vera's cheeks flushed and she blinked her eyes. "He knows this town and businesses that may have come and gone. I thought he might have some ideas."

She watched as the three ladies grinned at her. "What? He's a nice man... once you know how to *ask* him things."

Everyone laughed loudly, including Vera.

"If you think he has any ideas, by all means, ask him," Lainey chuckled. "We can use the help!"

"I'm meeting him for an early supper," Vera admitted.

Francy squinted her eyes and replied, "Do I need to remind you about curfews this evening? Or do I need to plan on another late night visit to the pokey?"

Lainey and Della burst out in laughter, not trying to hold it in. When Della caught her breath, she snorted, "Local Stink Bait Burglars strike again!"

Vera crossed her arms and looked annoyed. "Do you want our help or not?"

"Yes! Yes, we *do* want your help," Lainey managed to squeak out. She bit her lip trying to stop laughing.

"Okay, then. I'll ask him. But no promises."

"Well, I'd better get going. I want to catch Paul before he gets too busy," Della said as she stood up to leave. "I'll call you when he has the pictures ready."

"It's time for me to go, too," Vera stated. "I've got a hair appointment this afternoon." She looked to see the girls smiling. "It's my regular appointment... so stop grinning!"

Lainey nodded. "Thanks. Call me tomorrow if Shep has any information."

"Will do," Vera said, turning to face Francy. "Shep is picking me up. I'll call you in the morning."

Francy looked down, trying to keep herself from laughing. "Thanks for the night off, Mom."

Vera ignored the comment and continued out the door. Della followed behind her.

"Francy, you think we can go back to the dungeon now to look for articles on the Jackson's barn fire?"

"Let me see who's working today." She pulled out her cell phone, put it on speaker, and called the police station.

"Hello, Darlene. It's Francy. Anything special happening at the station today?"

"Hey. It's a bit slow today. Why?"

"I wanted to get into the dungeon and wondered if this afternoon was a good time?"

"Let me check." There were several minutes of silence.

"It looks like you were in the dungeon the other day. Didn't find what you were looking for?"

"It was so crazy with the fishing opener and the body investigation, I didn't have time to complete my research."

"I'll need to get this approved with Sarge. Hold on."

Lainey looked at Francy and frowned. "I was hoping he wouldn't be there."

Francy shrugged her shoulders. "He's going to have to know at some point."

Darlene came back on the phone. "Francy, Sarge says it's okay. But stop at his office first. He said to come before 2 p.m."

"Will do. Thanks."

Lainey looked at her watch. "We've got about an hour. Let's go by Babe's and bring him a coffee and maybe a piece of pie."

"Probably a good idea. His favorite is coconut cream. I'll drive so we don't have two cars."

Lainey agreed. They put the old newspapers back in their folders.

"He's going to want to see these. Are you going to tell him about the pictures Della has?" Francy asked.

"I'm not sure. Let's see what his mood is today."

The two left Lainey's and drove to the coffee house to pick up their delicious bribe for Sarge. It wasn't long before Francy was parking in the rear parking lot of the police station. They got out of her car and walked to the back door. Darlene buzzed them in and when the door opened, Sarge was waiting for them.

"Hello, ladies," Sarge stated. "I thought you might need an escort to my office in case you got lost."

Lainey shrugged her shoulders and smiled. "We come bearing gifts!" She raised the Babe's plastic bag and cup of coffee for him to see.

Sarge's expression didn't change. He turned around and walked toward his office. "Follow me."

Francy glanced at Lainey with a somewhat worried look on her face. "Looks like the bear is in today."

"I know. Darn it. I'm going to have to tell him everything I have so far."

They walked into Sarge's office to find him standing behind his desk, waiting for them to sit in the two chairs directly in front of him. They sat down and then he sat down.

"Lainey, how many times have I told you that you need to keep me in the loop? Especially if you are investigating on your own."

Lainey cringed a little bit. "Sarge, I had an appointment scheduled with you for earlier this morning, but we got held up at the museum."

"She's right, Sarge," Francy added. "We spent more time there than we had planned."

Sarge leaned back in his chair, resting his arms across his stomach. He squinted his eyes, looking first at Lainey, then to Francy. Suddenly, he raised his arms and clasped his hands behind his head.

"How is Agnes?"

Lainey glanced at Francy. "Well, she's a wonderfully sweet lady. She told us so much about the museum."

Sarge nodded but said nothing.

"It's been a long time since I was in the museum, but Mrs. Mitchell gave us a very informative tour," Francy said.

Sarge was still silent.

Okay, I'll wait you out, Sarge. I hope Francy doesn't say anything else until he speaks first.

Francy knew to keep quiet until spoken to. She didn't want to fall into the trap of giving up too much information.

After a few more minutes of silence, Sarge put his hands down and sat up straight in his chair.

"Darlene says you want back in the dungeon."

"Yes, sir," Francy started. "We'd like to look at the boat pictures again. With all the action going on that night, we didn't get to examine them as closely as we'd like."

"I see."

"Have you gotten any reports back from the coroner on the identification of the body?" Lainey asked, trying to put him back on the spot.

Sarge leaned forward, folding his hands together on top of his desk. "This is the same song and dance we play on every case. I want to know what you've found. What questions do you have?"

Lainey shrugged. "You're right. There are so many things that I can't completely pin down."

"For example?"

"How did the boat sink? Was there a hole in it? Did the

person commit suicide or was he handcuffed to it and murdered?"

"First, let me say that we don't have the DNA results back, so I can't say whether it was a he or she. Secondly, the investigation showed no holes large enough to have caused the boat to sink. We did find that the drain plug was missing."

Francy crossed her legs in the chair. "A drain plug can sink a boat?"

Sarge nodded. "It happens all the time. When the boat is moving forward, the front end is higher than the rear. Water collected from waves or water spray exits the boat through the drain at the rear of the boat. It's about deck level. Once you stop moving, if that drain isn't plugged, water continues to come in and will sink the boat."

"It's murder, then, isn't it?" Lainey asked.

"Or possibly suicide."

Francy looked at Lainey. "Tell him what we know about that boat."

"The name of the boat, *A Gemelos Dream*, was the name of a boat owned by Martin Jackson."

Sarge took a deep breath and sighed. "We've been researching that. What makes you think so?"

"Aggie confirmed it for us. She said that Martin used to store that boat in one of her family's barns during the winter months. She had to clean it. She remembers the name clearly."

"I've been so busy, I hadn't thought to check with Aunt Aggie."

"*Aunt Aggie?* She's your aunt?" Francy sputtered.

"Yes, by marriage. If she says it's Jackson's boat, then I believe her." He pulled out a pad and pen and began making notes. "I need to look into this right away."

He looked up to dismiss the two ladies, and noticed Lainey was squirming in her chair. "There's more?"

"I think there could be, but I don't have enough proof to…" Lainey began.

"Maynard, tell me what you know… *now!*"

Man! I hate to show my hand to him without proof!

Lainey sighed heavily and began telling Sarge her ideas.

"You know that Melvin Jackson was a twin. Larry Jackson was the one who was driving when Beverly Daschel was killed."

Sarge's eyes narrowed. "Yes. I'm aware of that case. What else?"

"Larry disappeared before he could be tried. The family's boat disappeared about the same time." She pulled out the newspaper articles showing the wrecked car and handed them to Sarge. "According to Aggie, some people thought he sunk the boat and ran away to Canada. Others have thought he committed suicide."

He thumbed through the pages of the paper. "You're thinking Larry's body was found in the boat?"

"No, sir, I don't."

Sarge stared at her. "You don't?"

Before Lainey could answer, dispatch paged him. "Sir, there's a 10-54. Officer requesting assistance."

"10-4," Sarge answered. "We will continue this when I get back." He left the office quickly with Lainey and Francy still sitting in the chairs.

"How'd you think he took that news?" Francy asked.

"I can never tell with him. Let's get to the dungeon before he gets back to change his mind."

They walked quickly to the old records room. Once inside, Francy logged into the computer.

"Now that we know the drain plug was missing, what are we looking for?"

"Can we find any reports of stolen property or vandalism at that old mine? You know, the Hill Annex Mine. The one in the picture?" Lainey asked. "Are we allowed to open any of these evidence boxes?"

"There should be pictures on this computer of everything that is put into an evidence box. What are you looking for?"

"I don't know, but anything about crimes at that old mine would be a good start."

Francy spent the next hour searching through files while Lainey paced back and forth, staring at the rows and rows of evidence boxes sitting on the shelves. She walked through the narrow aisles, hoping to find some code or name that might link it to the abandoned mine.

"Without some date or more specific information, I'm afraid we're not going to find anything on this computer," Francy said. She sat back in the little chair and frowned.

"Thanks for checking. Let's get out of this dungeon and grab a bite to eat."

"Agreed. I'm starving. How about a Subway sandwich?" She shut off the computer and the two left the room and headed to the parking lot.

"Wonder if Della has found anything," Francy said as she unlocked her car. "Maybe worth a call to see?"

Lainey nodded. She got into the car and pulled her cell phone out of her pocket. She dialed Della but got no answer. During the failed phone call, Francy had pulled into the Subway drive through and was ordering a meatball sub with everything on it. Lainey ordered a spicy Italian sub with extra spicy mustard.

"Let's go to the park and eat," Francy said. "Looking at the trees helps me to clear my mind sometimes."

Lainey agreed and they drove a few miles to Turkey Creek Park. It was one of the newer park areas in town. It wasn't large but had a new play area for kids and several covered picnic tables. They parked, rolled down their windows, and ate in Francy's car.

"I didn't realize I was this hungry," Francy said as she finished her sandwich. "That was really good."

"I know. Wish I'd ordered lemonade, but water is good, too."

Francy paused for a moment. "You haven't told me what you think. I've been guessing, but I want to know."

"Don't you think it's odd that Quincy Yelnick was in a picture with Melvin and a young Marvin? I mean, even if it were a photo stunt or opportunity, why was Yelnick there?"

"Good question. I don't have an answer for you."

Lainey paused as she pulled her thoughts together. "Something bothers me about Aggie's description of Melvin after his brother's disappearance. I wonder if twins take on the personality of the other if one dies?"

Francy shrugged her shoulders. "I've always thought Melvin Jackson was a soft spoken man who tried to manipulate people and the press to get what he wanted. But he did show another side of himself at the drawing for the fish opener."

"Yes, he did indeed. Another thing is bothering me, though. If Marvin saw the sunken boat and body before I arrived, before the tarp was put over it, wouldn't he have seen the name of the boat?"

Francy perked up as if a light bulb went off over her head. "Of course! He would have told his dad the name of the boat. Marvin would have *known* it was his family's boat!"

"That's what I think. But how can we prove that? I think I may need to meet with good old Marvin again. I need to know what he really saw."

"Better take a backup with you this time."

"I agree. I need a better way to meet with him. I'll come up with something." Lainey looked at her watch. "How about we drive to Della's and see if she's found anything."

"Sounds good. Maybe Paul has those photos enlarged, too."

Francy started the car, backed out of the parking lot, and headed to Della's house.

CHAPTER 13

Della was sitting on her front porch swing drinking coffee when Francy pulled into the driveway. She waved at the two as they got out of the car.

"I thought you might be coming over here," Della said. "I saw you called earlier." She scooted to one side of the swing, motioning for the ladies to sit down.

"It's a gorgeous evening," Francy commented. "Wish I had a swing like this."

"I wish it was on the back patio, but Paul says it gets more sunlight here."

"Where is Paul?" Lainey asked, sitting between the two.

"He's inside loading the dishwasher."

"Wow... you've trained him well!" Francy grinned.

Della chuckled. "We have an agreement, if he cooks, I clean. If I cook, he cleans. Works pretty well."

The three silently swung back and forth for a few minutes. Della took a sip of coffee before she spoke.

"Paul has the pictures inside, if that's the reason you came by."

"Great! It's part of the reason," Lainey began. "Were you

able to find anything that might connect Melvin, Quincy, or the mine?"

"That gets a bit complicated. I've made notes and printed out some things for you. Let's go inside."

Francy and Lainey followed Della inside. Paul was sitting at the kitchen bar, munching on a hearty slice of Vera's banana nut bread.

"Hello, ladies," Paul said between bites. "Tell Vera this bread is amazing."

Francy smiled, shot a quick glance at Della, then winked. "I'm glad you're enjoying it. I'll tell her."

Lainey pulled up a stool and sat next to him. "Thank you for working on those pictures. I'm eager to see them."

Paul smiled and gulped down the last bite of bread. "They're on my desk. I'll get them for you."

Della and Francy were sitting at the dining room table. Lainey could hear them discussing the information Della had printed off her computer.

"It looks like Melvin and Quincy have been partners in at least a couple of business ventures over the years," Della began. "I wonder if Lainey has talked with Mr. Hughes, yet?"

"Do you mean the Dewayne Hughes that retired from law enforcement?" Francy questioned.

Lainey frowned and said aloud, "Shoot! I completely forget about calling Mr. Hughes."

"Why don't we give him a call now?" Paul asked. "I'm betting he would welcome the company."

He reached into his pants pocket for his cell phone and used his voice command, "Call Brookshire Senior Living Center." It wasn't long before a female voice answered and directed his call to Dewayne's room. It wasn't on speaker and Lainey could only hear Paul's side of the conversation.

"Hello, Dewayne! It's Paul Kristiansen." There was a pause

before he spoke again. "Yes, sir, Della is fine. I was hoping you might feel up to having a couple of visitors?"

Paul looked at Lainey and grinned. "I wanted to bring a couple friends of ours with me. Do you remember Francy Baines?" Paul nodded silently. "The other person is Lainey Maynard. She's extremely interested in talking with you about your time at the police station." Again, Paul paused. This time his smile turned into a straight line. "They do have questions about evidence from a possible cold case. Would you mind talking with us?"

Lainey, Della, and Francy were pacing behind Paul's chair, listening and trying not to make a sound. After what seemed like an eternity, Paul nodded once more and said, "Thank you, Dewayne. We will see you in a short while." He ended the call and turned to look at the ladies who were staring at him anxiously.

"He said we could come now, but he sounded a little bit...disappointed."

"Disappointed?" Della asked. "Why?"

Paul shrugged his shoulders. "Maybe because we aren't coming just to visit him. We want something from him."

Francy sighed. "He sat in the dungeon every day taking pictures, labeling boxes, and trying to learn the computer systems. People came in that room only if they needed something. Very few people went just to see how he was."

Della walked over to the cabinet. "Paul, is he still on a gluten free diet? I think I may have some cookies left that we could take over there."

"I think he'd appreciate that. And I'll make a point to visit him more often. But now, let's get going. The Senior center closes to visitors at 9 p.m."

Paul grabbed the folder containing the pictures and headed to the garage. "We'll need to take separate cars. Della, bring what information you have. I have the photos."

Paul's car led the way and he parked close to the visitor's entrance of Brookshire Senior Living Center. Lainey and Francy parked next to him. They got out of their cars and Paul gathered them together briefly.

"Let me buzz the front desk. Dewayne's room is in the independent living wing, but we have to walk through the marketplace. The doors between wings are on a timer, so stay fairly close together. I don't want the door to close on someone."

They nodded and followed Paul. He buzzed and the security guard at the front desk opened the door after checking his list of visitors. The single story building was nice, and the guard's desk was located in the middle of what was called the Market Place Street. The inside walls were faux brick and had several storefronts along them. Tall, white, lamp posts were located along the walkway that led into a four-square area. There were several park benches and large potted plants placed along the square. A street sign pointed to each side of the square and listed the name of the wing in that direction.

"My goodness," Francy commented. "There's a grocery store, a beauty salon, a restaurant, and fitness room in this area."

"The idea is to have a market square where residents, if able, can visit without having to drive or take a city bus," Della answered. "I think it's a great idea. There's a wood shop and craft area, too."

"I love these lamp posts," Lainey remarked. "They look like they came straight from a London park street corner!"

"We'd better get going. The independent wing is on our right," Paul said. He walked to the large double doors and rang the bell on the outside. Another voice asked him to identify himself and the person he was to visit. The door clicked and the four went inside.

Della walked up beside Paul and put her arm through his. "I'm here for you, dear. We haven't visited since we lost your mom."

Paul patted her hand and smiled. "Thank you, sweetie. I'm okay."

Francy and Lainey followed the two down the wide hallway.

"It's just like a hotel or apartment building," Francy said. "Some doors have decorations on them. Some have plant stands and flowers sitting next to them. This one has a name plate on it."

"It's their front porch, so to speak," Lainey smiled. "I like it. I'd make mine welcoming, too."

Paul stopped in front of room 227 and rang the doorbell. A tall, slender man opened the door.

"Hello, Paul. It's good to see you. Won't you come in?"

Paul hugged the man. "It's good to see you, Dewayne. You're still looking fit my man."

Dewayne laughed. "Good genes, I guess. Your bride is as beautiful as ever."

Della blushed and hugged him. "You're just the sweetest thing. Good to see you."

Francy and Lainey walked in behind her.

"Why, Francy Baines," Dewayne said loudly, "I heard you finally retired. Good to see you!"

"I don't know how they are running the station without us," Francy laughed as she hugged him. "You never change. Good looking as ever."

"And who is your friend?"

"I'm Lainey Maynard. It's nice meeting you, sir." She put out her hand to shake his. He hugged her instead.

"If they consider you a friend, then I do too." He grinned. "Let's go into the living room and sit down."

Della and Paul sat on the couch while Francy and Lainey

sat down in recliners that were on each end. Dewayne's chair, a larger Lazy-Z Boy with pristine looking leather, sat with its back to the kitchen bar.

"I like sitting here," he began. "I can watch television or watch the world go by from my picture window."

"Your home is lovely," Lainey said. "My cat would love the fireplace."

"It's one of those gas ones," he chuckled. "Guess they don't trust us old fogeys with a wood burning stove."

They all laughed. Paul was the first to speak.

"Dewayne, we're here to ask you about the car accident that killed little Beverly Daschel. Did you work the evidence for that one?"

"That was one of the tragic ones," he began. "My role in the department was to process every piece of evidence." He shook his head sadly. "There is so much violence in this world. Unfortunately, I saw all of it in our jurisdiction. Yes, I remember the case."

Paul looked at Lainey and motioned for her to talk.

"Mr. Hughes," she began.

"Please, call me Dewayne."

"Dewayne, I don't quite know where to begin," Lainey stammered, glancing at Paul for help. "Are you aware of the sunken boat and the body that was found the morning of the fishing opener?"

"My brother attended the big drawing ceremony. He told me about it."

"I have a hunch, nothing official, but I think that body may be tied in some way to the car accident that killed Beverly." She waited for some kind of response or movement from the man but saw nothing.

No more beating around the bush, Lainey. Spit it out and see what happens.

"Do you think that Larry Jackson killed himself in order to avoid being convicted of murder?" she blurted out.

Dewayne blinked a couple of times, then wrinkled his mouth from side to side. "Are you investigating this as a cold case?"

"No, sir. I am an investigator, but I'm not officially assigned to this case. I have worked with Sarge and the police department for more than ten years."

"The girls were working the fishing opener," Paul explained, "and were at the Backwater during the recovery operation. I've known Lainey for a long time. Her gut feelings or intuitions are usually spot on."

"I haven't seen where the body has been identified," Dewayne stated. "Are you thinking the body is the Jackson boy?"

Lainey thought for a moment before speaking. She shot a glance and nodded at Francy.

"We know that the boat belonged to Martin Jackson," Francy said. "Although, this is strictly off the record."

"I see. And what proof do you have?"

"There was a name on the side of the boat," Lainey answered. "*The Gemelos Dream*. We have someone who was familiar with the boat and has confirmed it."

Paul opened the envelope he carried and pulled out the pictures he had blown up. "We're hoping you might know of any connections between Melvin Jackson and Quincy Yelnick." He handed the picture of the men taken at the mine.

Dewayne took a long look at the photo. "They were young men back then, must be late 80's or early 90's." He pulled the photo closer to study it. "See that small logo on Quincy's shirt?"

Paul took the picture back and looked closely. "I didn't see that!"

Lainey fidgeted in her chair. "What logo? I haven't seen these since you enlarged them."

"Take a look," Paul replied, handing her the picture. "Wasn't that a trucking company?"

Francy walked over to stand behind Lainey and look at the photo. Sure enough, there was a logo on the front pocket of Quincy's shirt.

"J. Y. Transports," Dewayne said. "Jackson Yelnick Transportation. If I remember correctly, Melvin and Quincy were partners in a small trucking company transporting farm supplies."

"Della, can you do some internet research on the company?" Lainey asked. "I'd like to know who the partners were and how long they were in business."

"There were only two partners," Dewayne smiled. "Melvin made the business connections and Yelnick drove the truck. They used to meet for coffee every Saturday morning at the old Sunray Truck Stop west of town. It was the hotspot back in the day."

He looked down and frowned just a bit. "Jackson always bragged loudly to make sure people heard all about his great business ventures. I overheard them many times. The business ran into financial trouble."

Lainey was watching him closely as he spoke. While his face was pleasant, she noticed that he had begun to tap his right heel ever so slightly on the carpet when he mentioned the business partners. She knew something about this made him uncomfortable.

"Dewayne, do you remember any lawsuits filed or any criminal charges against J. Y. Transports?" she cautiously asked him.

He took a moment to look at her and think about his answer. Lainey saw his hesitation and quickly tried to smooth over any discomfort.

"I know you are highly respected in this community. My question wasn't meant to make you feel uncomfortable. If you have any information that could help, I would greatly appreciate it."

The man took a deep breath and let it out slowly. "Everyone has secrets in a small town, Lainey. Some people are incredibly good at covering them up, others are not."

Dewayne uncrossed his legs and stood up. He stretched his arms above his head, then put them down resting his hands on his waist.

"Are you saying Melvin and Quincy covered up something?" Francy asked suddenly. Lainey shot a surprised glance her way, hoping she hadn't blurted out too much too soon.

"I miss you, Francy," he said as he sat back down. "We had a good long run down at the station, didn't we?"

"Yes, sir," she chuckled. "Some of the best and worst people passed through our office."

"I'm not sure you were employed at the station when Melvin and Yelnick came to traffic court, but I was the court bailiff at the time."

"I had no idea! What happened?"

"Yelnick had been ticketed for parking and storing his truck illegally behind an abandoned farm supply building. It was clearly posted as private property. The owners found his truck parked behind the building several times. They reported it to the police, who issued one citation after another. Finally, after a dozen or so tickets, Yelnick was picked up and brought to jail."

Paul cleared his throat and nodded. "I remember the scandal around Mirror Falls when Melvin showed up to post bail for him. Didn't he take the local news photographer with him to the jail?"

Dewayne nodded. "Along with two reporters and our

radio DJ. Jackson never missed a chance to get his name in the paper or have people think he was being mistreated. Chet Parsons, the jailer at the time, was on duty when they showed up. He said Melvin was crowing like a rooster about police brutality. The photographer was snapping photos wildly and the flashbulbs blinded him. Both reporters shoved microphones in his face, trying to get an exclusive. He said he felt like bait being dangled above a tank of starving muskies."

"I didn't think photos could be taken inside a jail." Lainey said.

"That's true. The jail was a separate building then, located a couple of blocks away from the station. At the time, only one jailer was on duty for each shift. Chet was a sitting duck."

"Thankfully, security measures to protect jailers has changed a great deal," Francy said. "It would take an order from the governor to get into the jail these days. What happened when they appeared in court?"

"Yelnick got out on bail and a court hearing date was set for a few days later. We figured they would show up, try to contest the tickets, then pay their fine and leave."

Paul looked around the room. "I remember hearing about the brawl on the radio. Melvin made sure it got little notice in the local newspaper. Not one article was written about it."

"Brawl? There was a fight in the courtroom?" Della asked.

"Yes, Ma'am," Dewayne replied. "Melvin didn't hire an attorney. He fully intended to defend his partner himself. He arrived at the courthouse a good hour early to get his presentation in order. Yelnick was supposed to arrive shortly before the hearing began."

"*Supposed* to arrive?" Francy asked. "He didn't show?"

"He did show up...fifteen minutes late and drunk as a skunk. Melvin tried to keep him quiet, but Yelnick kept spewing loud insults about the judge and the town. The judge warned him several times to keep quiet, but Yelnick continued. Before the judge put the two of them in jail for contempt of court, Melvin decked him."

Lainey's mouth flew open. "He punched him?"

"He knocked him out cold," Dewayne chuckled. "Jackson had a wicked right hand punch."

"What did the judge do?"

"He fined Melvin for disrupting the proceedings and sentenced both to jail time if they didn't pay the traffic tickets and get out of his courtroom. It wasn't long after that J. Y. Transport went out of business."

Della was shaking her head in disbelief. "I wouldn't have thought Mayor Jackson could throw a punch let alone knock out a bully like Quincy Yelnick."

Lainey began feeling that familiar tingling sensation on her skin and thoughts were racing through her mind about their encounter with him at the fishing opener.

"Francy, didn't Sarge tell us that Yelnick owned a convenience store chain in this area?"

"Yes, he owns a few *Dip and Chip* convenience stores."

"I wonder if he had or has any partners?"

Dewayne smiled. "Jackson was his partner for a while. Then he sold his interest."

"To whom?" Lainey asked.

"Marvin Jackson."

CHAPTER 14

The surprise on Francy's face was unmistakable. She glanced at Lainey who was grinning slyly from ear to ear.

"They certainly keep things in the family, don't they?" Della remarked, looking at Paul in disbelief. "What else do the Jackson's have their hands in?"

Dewayne looked down and smiled. "It's a small town, my friend. A ridiculously small town."

Lainey stood up, still smiling broadly. "Thank you for inviting us into your home. You have no idea how much you have helped us."

"It's my pleasure," he answered. "I hope you will visit again and come for supper. I make a mean vegetarian lasagna. And it's been a while since I've had guests."

"I'm in!" Francy said raising her hand up. "I've tasted his lasagna...it's to die for!"

"Count us in, too," Della said, pulling Paul up from his seat on the couch.

"That sounds like a plan," Lainey said.

Dewayne opened the door, hugged the ladies as they

walked past and shook Paul's hand. Once in the hallway, he called out to Francy. "Does your Mom still make those coconut cream chocolate bars? The ones with marshmallows?"

Francy turned and smiled. "She sure does. I'll see if she can make some for you."

"Thanks. I miss the treats she used to bring to the station. And let's face it, store bought cookies can't touch her baking!"

The minute the group was outside in the parking lot, they circled around Lainey and all talked at once.

"What do you know?" "Why are you smiling?" "Would you fill me in here?"

Lainey couldn't figure out who was saying what. She raised her hand in the air.

"Wait a second! The three of you are surrounding me like vultures hovering over the newest roadkill."

Paul sighed. "You're right. This is not the place to talk. Lainey, your house is close by, can we go there and discuss this?"

"We can, but it's pretty late…"

"Oh no…I want to hear what's running around in your head, my friend," Francy interrupted.

"Okay, okay. Let's meet at my house."

They nodded to each other, got in their cars, and followed closely behind Lainey's car. She pulled into her garage and got out to meet them.

"Let's sit on the patio," Lainey said. "It's a nice evening and this won't take much time."

The four walked around to her backyard and sat down at the small patio table.

"Paul," Lainey began. "Can I see the photo of the Jackson twins? The one you enlarged?"

He nodded and opened the envelope. He pulled out both

photos and pushed the one of the twins toward her. She picked it up, studied it for a moment, and put it on the table.

"For Pete's sake, tell us what you're thinking," Francy stated. "Why is this photo important?"

"I'm asking you to be patient with me. I don't have any real evidence, just hunches. But for tonight, I want you to look at this picture once more. Focus on the twins."

Each one took their turn looking at the picture. When they had finished, Lainey continued.

"Paul, would you please make several more copies of this enlarged picture? And the one at the mine? I'd like to take them with me when I talk to Sarge tomorrow morning."

"Sure. But what are we looking for?"

"They look identical to me," Della remarked. "I mean, from this photo, you can't really tell one from the other."

"What about you, Francy? Any comments on that picture?" Lainey asked.

"I don't know which twin is which, but the one on the left appears to be a little bulkier. I mean more muscular or something. Maybe it's just the camera angle."

"I thought so too."

Paul picked up the photo again and nodded. "You know, I think you're right. One does appear a bit heavier than the other one."

"I can't tell you anything more tonight," Lainey continued. "And I'm sorry to keep you wondering. I think these two pictures are connected to the death of Beverly Daschel, Larry's disappearance, and the body in the boat. Until I have solid proof and Sarge is involved, I can't take the chance of putting any of you in harm's way."

"It is late," Paul said. "And I agree. Until you have proof, speculation won't help anyone. I'll have those copies ready for you by 7 a.m. Want to come by the house to pick them up?"

"Thanks, Paul. I'll be there no later than 7:30."

"Okay. Della, my sweet, let's go home. I think there is a little bit of Vera's banana nut bread left and it's calling my name."

They got up and hugged Lainey goodbye. Francy, who remained seated at the table, waited until the two had gone before she leaned forward and looked Lainey straight in the eye.

"You're not going to the station without me. And I'm not leaving until you level with me."

"Francy, I'm not going to meet with Sarge in the morning."

"Why am I not surprised? Where are you going?"

"*We* are going back to the museum basement. I want to talk with Aggie."

"And that's all?"

"No. We're going to open that old garage entry and see what's inside."

"I don't think Aggie will agree to that."

"That's why we need Vera to come with us and bring goodies to share with her over tea."

"Great idea! While they're upstairs, we'll be in the basement."

"Exactly. Can you call her this late and find out if she'll help?"

Francy rolled her eyes and laughed. "Are you kidding? Since Mom's been seeing Shep, anything before midnight is early! I'll call her on my way home."

Lainey chuckled. "And if she's not home yet?"

"Good grief! I never dreamed I'd be grounding my mother for staying out too late!"

Both giggled for a long time.

"Okay. Let's meet at the museum a little before 8 in the morning," Lainey said.

"We will be there. Anything else I should bring?"

"Do you still have the portable shovel? You know the one you used to carry in your trunk in the winter?"

"I never go anywhere without it. I have a couple of long handle flashlights, too."

"Sounds good. I have gardening gloves we can use, and I'll bring trash bags."

"Trash bags? What do you think we will find? And how big do you think it is?"

Lainey shrugged. "I don't know, but it's the only chance we have and I want to make sure whatever we find, we can carry it out."

Francy nodded and said goodbye. Lainey walked with her back to the driveway and waved as she drove off. She sighed and walked through the garage to the utility room door.

She opened the door to see a somewhat disgruntled cat sitting on top of the dryer meowing loudly. "Hey, Powie. I know it's late." She petted the cat who turned his head away as if ignoring her.

"Don't you give me attitude," she said playfully. "Let's get you some food."

Once she had taken care of the cat's needs, she changed into her pajamas and sat down at her computer. She turned it on and waited for it to boot up. Powie jumped into her lap after satisfying his hunger and began purring.

"Something keeps bothering me about the Jacksons and Yelnick being in partnership," she wondered aloud. "What did Melvin and Quincy have in common? How or why did they form a trucking company? And after all these years, why did Melvin get his son involved?"

She spent the next few hours scouring the internet for anything related to Jackson Yelnick Transport and the Dip and Chip convenience stores.

Lainey leaned back in her chair, raising her arms to

stretch. Her movement disturbed her cat's sleep and he gave a short *meow* and jumped down. She rubbed her forehead in frustration.

What am I missing? There must be a connection...

Suddenly she sat straight up in her chair and grinned. "Snoops! He can find out!"

She quickly unlocked her work server and emailed her favorite fellow employee. She wasn't surprised to get a call on her work phone within minutes of hitting the send button.

"Still working into the wee hours of the night, I see," the man's voice said when she answered.

"Clyde Bedlow, you know it's the best time to get things done. I learned my work ethic from the best."

He chuckled. "I do train people well, don't I? Your email said you're looking into a murder some years ago. What do you need from me?"

"Were you able to open those pictures I attached to the email?"

"I'm looking at them now."

"Our current Mayor is one of the twins standing on the football field in the first photo. And some twenty or more years later, he is the man standing on the far left in the second photo. His son is standing beside him. But the man I'm more interested in is standing behind those two. Do you see him?"

Snoops paused and she could hear him typing on his computer keyboard. "Your email said his name is Quincy Yelnick. Is that the one?"

"It sure is. I have a gut feeling that those three men have been involved in more things than just a photo opportunity at a mine."

"I see. By gut feeling, do you mean you've got proof?"

Lainey shrugged her shoulders and winced. "Not exactly. That's why I emailed you."

"I'm listening. Give me names, birthdates, and whatever else you have," he replied.

"It's a long story and a bit complicated," she said cautiously.

He laughed loudly. "It always is, my friend. It always is."

It took her fifteen minutes to tell him about the boat and sunken body, the fire, the Jackson's, and her encounter with Yelnick and Marvin.

"I'm afraid to ask," Snoops said. "Have you told the police about any of this?"

"Well,..." she heard him groan loudly. "I need evidence before I say anything."

"I'll see what I can locate on the transportation company and the convenience store partnerships. Are you aware of any legal issues these three have had?"

"Oh! Yes! I forgot about the court brawl between Quincy and Jackson. Quincy had many parking citations he had ignored. He was eventually arrested and a court date was determined. Jackson came to court to defend him. Seems Yelnick appeared at the proceeding late and drunk. He began berating and yelling at the judge. Jackson ended up knocking him out before the judge put them both in jail for contempt."

"That was the transportation company, right?"

"Yes. From what I was told, Jackson was the boss and Yelnick was the driver. But I think there's more to it."

"How comfortable are you with your source? Hearsay is not much to go on."

She grunted. "I spoke with the bailiff that was on duty when it happened. Would I mislead you on purpose?"

He was silent.

"One more thing, please. Do you still have access to coroner's records and medical files?"

"You want me to get a sneak peek at the DNA results for the body."

She smiled. "Exactly."

"No promises, but I'll see what I can find out."

"Thank you, Snoops. How're things going in the Houston office? Whose bringing you donuts now that I'm gone?"

"We have a newbie, fresh from college, who thinks he's Perry Mason."

"I see. Got to break him in the right way. The Bedlow way!"

He laughed. "Hopefully. He's not as hardheaded as one young female newbie was. She was still bringing me donuts years later."

"I take offense at that! I wasn't hardheaded! And the donuts were your favorite bribe!"

"My wife has me on some lose-weight-for-old-folks diet," he complained. "My only escape from the pink liquid protein drinks is my daily donut and coffee!"

"She cares about you, that's all. How much weight have you lost?"

He chuckled. "I've gained four pounds."

Lainey laughed so hard, her eyes began tearing up.

"It's getting late. How soon can you get me information? I want to get in touch with Sarge at the police station before the coroner's report hits the newspapers."

"Depends on how deep I have to search. Hopefully, I'll have something for you in the morning. Check your email."

"Great. Thank you, Snoops. You're still the best, even if you are a little bit portly!"

"Portly? Four pounds and now I'm portly?" he gave a fake gasp. "I'd rather die portly and full of donuts than skinny and full of pink fluid." He could hear her laughing.

"Sounds good. I appreciate this, my friend. Talk to you tomorrow."

She ended the call, turned off her computer, and got ready for bed. She tried to fall asleep, but thoughts of bodies, fires and sprinkled covered donuts keep swirling in her mind.

"Relax, Lainey. Breathe in deeply a few times. Tomorrow is waiting and you need to be on your toes," she thought to herself.

She dozed off and was awakened by her furry alarm cat precisely at 4 a.m. Slowly she got out of bed and stumbled half-asleep into the kitchen.

"Must you eat on the dot of 4 every morning?" she mumbled. Powie was purring loudly, waiting anxiously in front of his dish. She filled his bowl and gave him fresh water while her Keurig was warming up. She felt unusually tired this morning and made herself a large mocha frappe with extra dark chocolate.

"Ah, that tastes so good," she said aloud. "Wonder if I have anything from Snoops."

She took her coffee into her office and turned on the computer. She drank several bigger gulps before the email server was connected. Sure enough, an email was waiting for her. The subject line read *"For you to take to Sarge - asap."* There were three attachments.

Lainey began reading, nodding in agreement several times. She opened each attachment and saved them in a folder marked Ultimo Ganador. She printed each attachment and put them in a manilla folder to take to Sarge. If she was going to meet Francy and Vera at the museum at 8 a.m., she needed to get moving. She shut down her computer, showered, and dressed as quickly as possible. She was finishing up her last drink of coffee when her cell phone rang. It was Francy.

"Morning. Are you and Vera still coming to the museum?" she asked. "I'll bring you a caramel cinnamon roll if you like."

"Quincy Yelnick's been found dead. Sarge wants us at his office asap. I'll drive. Are you ready?"

Stunned, Lainey's mouth dropped open. "Dead? How? Yes, I'm dressed."

"Good, I'm on the way. I don't know much, but I'll fill you in as we drive."

She gathered her thoughts, grabbed the folder of the printed attachments from Snoops, and her backpack. Francy was pulling into her driveway as she hit the button to open the garage door. Lainey ran out to her car, got in, and closed her garage door.

"Quincy is dead?" she muttered, still a bit in shock.

"Yes. Maybe suicide."

"What happened?"

"I was up early, washing a load of laundry, when I heard the news on my scanner. All I know is that his body was found..." she paused and swallowed hard. "He was found behind the Backwater Restaurant. Before I could learn more, Sarge called."

They sat in stunned silence. Francy had pulled into the rear parking lot of the police station before either could speak.

Lainey looked at Francy, whose face had turned pale.

"Who found the body?" she asked quietly, although she already knew. A sharp pain ran through her core.

"Shep." Francy glanced at Lainey, her eyes moist with tears. "Shep found him."

Both fell silent. Neither one knowing what to say.

"We'd better go inside. Sarge is waiting," Francy said. She patted her eyes dry and got out of the car.

Lainey nodded and got out of the car. They walked toward the station's back entrance.

"Why would Sarge want us at the station? How did he sound when you talked to him?"

"I wouldn't say he was mad. He was definitely in cop mode."

The folder Lainey was holding suddenly felt as heavy as a concrete block. Francy hit the buzzer and the door opened. They walked down the hallway and into Sarge's office. He was sitting behind his desk, talking on the phone. He motioned for them to come in.

They sat in the two chairs in front of his desk.

"We'll be right there," Sarge hung up the phone. He saw the confusion and shocked look on the faces of both women. He let out a big sigh before he spoke.

"Shep is in the interrogation room and he's asking for you, Lainey."

Lainey thought she nodded her head, but she wasn't sure. It was all so surreal and she still couldn't believe what was happening.

"I'll take you to him," he said.

They walked quietly down the hallway, through the jail security, and stood in front of one of the interrogation rooms. Sarge knocked on the door. The officer inside opened it and the three entered. He closed the door after them.

Lainey's mouth went dry as she stared at the small, square table in front of her. Two empty chairs were on one side of the table. Shep was sitting in a grey folding chair on the other side. His wrists were handcuffed to the middle of the tabletop.

Oh, no! They think Shep killed him.

CHAPTER 15

Shep watched as Lainey and Francy sat down on the opposite side of the table. There was a terrible sadness in the air that seemed to make it hard to breathe. It was suffocating.

"Shep, I'm here. I don't know what's happened, but I'm here," Lainey said trying to sound brave. She reached out and put her hands over his cuffed wrists. "It's going to be okay."

He nodded and looked at Sarge who was standing beside Francy. Then he gazed into Lainey's eyes.

"I had a dream last night," he said quietly. "The body from the sunken boat talked to me."

Francy turned her head away from Shep so he could not see the tears that were forming in her eyes.

A wave of nausea washed over Lainey. She swallowed hard several times trying not to throw up.

"I believe you," she said. "What did it say?"

Shep paused as if he dreaded telling her.

"He repeated things over and over again," he dropped his head and fell silent.

Lainey tightened her grip on his cuffed wrists. "Tell me. I will believe you."

"The body kept saying *He knows me. I'm not who they think I am. He's waiting by the water.* It was real. I know what I saw and heard."

Sarge cleared his throat. "We received a phone call about a possible burglary at the Backwater. When we arrived, we searched around the area. Shep was found leaning over Yelnick's body. That's why he is here."

Francy stood up and paced back and forth.

Lainey was focused on Shep. "I believe you and I'm going to do all I can to help you."

He nodded. "Does Vera know I'm here?"

"No. I haven't called her this morning," Francy answered.

"Good. No need to worry her."

Sarge put his hand on Lainey's shoulder. "That's all for now. We'll talk in my office."

"I'm going to help you, Shep. I'll be back soon," she said squeezing his wrists one last time. "I know you haven't done anything wrong."

"Thank you. I knew if anyone would understand, it would be you."

Sarge motioned for the officer to open the door and the three walked out. Lainey shivered when she heard the metal door shut, knowing Shep was still cuffed and alone behind it. She followed Francy back down the hallway and into Sarge's office. They sat down again in front of his desk.

Sarge sat down in his chair and put his hands on his desk.

"Why do you have him in handcuffs? He's not a threat to anyone." Lainey questioned. "Unless you suspect him of murder?"

"Shep and Quincy had a heated argument early yesterday evening at the restaurant. They were yelling so loudly that people in the dining room overheard them. Witnesses said they were standing at the back of the dining room near the kitchen entry and arguing over a bad meat shipment. Apparently Shep demanded a refund and Quincy refused to give one."

"Mom was in the kitchen when it happened," Francy confessed. "She said Yelnick was still angry over not being able to park his boat the night before the fishing opener. So, to get even with Shep, he shipped him over three hundred pounds of spoiled meat."

"I remember that incident," Lainey said. "I thought Yelnick was going to get violent with Della. When I saw the shotguns in the backseat of his car, I went to get Sarge."

Francy frowned. "He did say something about telling Shep his supply of free meat was over."

Sarge sighed. "The argument escalated and the two continued to bark at each other while they walked through the dining room. As Yelnick was about to leave through the front entrance, Shep shoved him into the wall."

"That doesn't prove Shep killed him," Lainey stated.

Sarge hesitated. "We have witnesses that heard Shep tell Quincy several times that he would kill him before paying him."

Lainey's face turned pale. Francy stood up to pace again.

"Look, I like Shep. Both men are known to have bad tempers." He rubbed his forehead with his right hand. "When we found Shep, he was holding the gun that killed Quincy. I have to keep him here."

Lainey had been rubbing her hand over the top of the folder she was still clutching. She knew Shep was telling the truth and she felt she was holding the way to prove it. She slowly raised the folder from her lap and put it on his desk.

"What's this?" Sarge asked.

"I asked Clyde Bedlow from my office to check on a

couple of hunches that I had. This is the information he found just this morning."

"I've talked with Clyde in the past. He's a smart man," Sarge commented as he reached for the folder. Lainey held up her hand to stop him.

"Wait. Before you look inside, there's a couple of things you need to know." She looked at Francy and motioned for her to stop pacing and sit down.

Sarge picked up the folder and opened it anyway. He pulled out the contents and laid them on his desktop without looking at them. "I'm waiting."

"From the moment the body was pulled from the sunken boat, I felt there was more going on than we knew. Francy and I talked to Shep while you were supervising the recovery team. He told me about his dreams... and how people thought he was crazy."

Sarge nodded. "I'm aware of the stories."

"I believe him, Sarge. I believe he saw a vision of the body and the boat that night. Through the years, I've had things like that happen to me." She paused to take a deep breath. "Most people thought I was a nut. I know from experience that it isn't fun to be the brunt of your hometown's jokes."

Francy had been sitting quietly watching for any reaction on Sarge's face. She knew he was not on board with the psychic dream stories. She had to step in before he stopped listening to Lainey.

"I need a drink of water. I'm going to bring you both back drinks, too."

"Thanks, Francy. I could use coffee right about now," Sarge responded.

"Me, too," Lainey said. She watched Francy leave the room, then turned back around to face Sarge.

"Look, we know that Melvin Jackson had a twin brother, Larry. I asked you about the car accident and the death of

Beverly Daschel, remember?" she stated strongly. She leaned forward and put her arms on his desk, hoping to convey the seriousness of what she was saying.

"We did talk about that. How does that tie in?"

"I think that Larry's disappearance, the body in the boat, and Yelnick are connected."

Sarge's eyes opened wider. "Where's your proof?"

She looked down at the papers. "In front of you."

He picked up the first document in the stack of papers and began to read. As he read, he said, "I see Mr. Bedlow had access to the as yet unpublished DNA report."

"Yes. You know the boat belonged to Martin Jackson."

He put down the paper and picked up the next one in the stack. "We are aware of that. You told me when we discussed this a few days ago, you didn't believe Larry Jackson was the body in the boat. This DNA report appears to prove otherwise."

"I asked Clyde to research how the DNA of identical twins could be different. His comments are on page two of the report."

Sarge flipped to the second page and read. He blinked a couple of times, then looked at her.

"If this is correct, the only way to accurately determine identity is through finger printing. Lainey, you know that's not possible. The body was a skeleton. There is no way to fingerprint it."

She took a breath and blew it out as if she were whistling. "Did you know that shortly after Larry disappeared, Melvin's personality changed? Several people noticed it. Are you aware of a fire that happened at Martin Jackson's farm about the same time?"

"I didn't know Melvin back then, so I can't speak to any personality changes. Why does the fire make a difference?"

"There is a newspaper article in the folder. It has a picture of the barn burning. And a later article talks about Melvin getting burned trying to put out that fire."

Sarge searched the remaining papers and read the newspaper clip. "It says it burned his hands."

Lainey sat back in her chair and crossed her arms.

"And there is one difference in identical twins. It's in their fingerprints. I don't think that's a coincidence."

Sarge raised his eyebrows and ever so slightly, nodded his head.

"Take a look at the photos. See the one with the twin boys?"

He picked up the photo and studied it. "It's the Jackson twins."

"It was taken when the high school got a new scoreboard. Martin Jackson wanted his sons to be noticed. I think the twin on the left has a larger build than the twin on the right. Do you agree?"

"Maybe. One could have been more of an athlete than the other. Where are you going with this?"

"Now look at the second photo. It was taken at the Hill Annex Mine after it became a state park."

"It's Melvin and his son, Marvin." He suddenly pulled the photo closer to his eyes. "That's Yelnick behind them."

Lainey nodded. "Yep. Paul, Della, Francy and I talked with Dewayne Hughes. He is a wonderful man by the way. He told us about a trucking company, Jackson Yelnick Transportation. Melvin and Yelnick were the only partners."

"I'm guessing Dewayne told you about the infamous courtroom battle between Jackson and Yelnick. Their company went belly up after that."

"Within three months' time, they were partners again in the Dip and Chip convenience stores. Jackson was the money behind it and Yelnick's job was to run it."

Sarge noticed another photo that had stuck to the back of

a piece of paper. He pulled it loose and found a second photo stuck to it. As he studied the new photos, Lainey watched his jaw drop. She couldn't help but smile.

He stared at them for several minutes. Both were black and white photos that had faded a bit with age. He closed his mouth and the longer he looked at the photos, the harder his jaw set. He was grinding his teeth like an angry bulldog when Francy returned.

"Hey, what's going on?" she noticed immediately Sarge's expression. He was livid.

"Who else has seen these?" he asked Lainey.

"Just you and me." She grinned. "I think I know a way to solve this, but I need you to help me. Will you do that?"

He put the photos carefully back into the envelope. "I will keep this safe for now. What do you need me to do?"

"I planned to get into the old basement entrance of the museum this morning," she said. "Vera is ready to run interference for us. I need you to go with me."

He nodded. "I'm asking you again, has anyone else seen these photos? I don't want any more surprises."

"No, sir. I haven't told anyone my thoughts. Ask Francy."

"She's right. It's been so frustrating!" she grinned.

"All right. What time do I meet you?"

"It's already open. Are you able to go now?" Lainey replied.

"The sooner the better. Let's go in my vehicle."

"No, that might draw too much attention. Gossips will see us getting out of your police cruiser and rumors will fly. Can you ride with us this time?"

He grimaced. "Who's driving?"

Francy sheepishly raised her hand. "We came in my car. I'm driving."

"Lord help us!" Sarge smiled. "Maynard, did you know

she had more speeding tickets than any other law enforcement employee in the history of the department?"

"It wasn't my fault. The guys thought it was fun to trap me. They didn't have to write a ticket every time!"

Lainey smiled, thankful for a little bit of respite from the seriousness of the moment.

"I'm riding shotgun, Baines. You may be retired, but I'm still your boss."

She laughed. "Yes, sir. If you're nice, I might just come out of retirement to be your personal driver!"

They walked out of his office, through the back entrance, to her car in the parking lot. Within a few minutes they were sitting in front of the museum. To their surprise, Vera was sitting in her car waiting for them.

"I've been waiting here for an hour!" she fumed as she got out of the car. "My cranberry puffs are getting cold!"

Francy grinned. "Mom, we got held up at the station. I didn't think you would come without me."

"You said I was to run interference for you at 8 a.m. I take my job seriously!"

Sarge laughed. "Vera, I'm sure whatever you made tastes great, hot or cold."

She grinned and gave him a hug. "You're still my favorite officer."

The group started walking toward the museum, but Vera stopped them.

"Wait a minute. Why is he here?" She shot a fiery glance toward Francy and pointed her first finger at her. "Francine Baines, you have not been honest with me! What's going on?"

"Vera, I decided to come because I haven't seen Aunt Aggie in some time. I'm just tagging along in case they need help in the basement," Sarge said trying to smooth things over.

"Well, if you say so. But I don't want to be left out of any exciting burglary stuff!"

Francy rolled her eyes. "Mom, we are not stealing anything."

They walked to the front door and knocked. As before, the delightful Aggie Mitchell greeted them. "Why, Ben! It's good to see you. How's your family?"

Sarge gave her a big hug. "Hello, Aunt Aggie. It's been too long since we've gotten together. The family is doing fine."

"Vera Abernathy! What a pleasant surprise. You're looking wonderful."

"Hello, Aggie. You haven't changed one bit. I'm just getting older and crotchetier!"

Aggie smiled. "Francy, I see you brought you friend back. Lainey Maynard, wasn't it?"

"Yes, Ma'am. I'm awfully glad to see you again."

"I wish I had known you were coming. I would have baked something for you."

"Aggie, do you still have that beautiful parlor room upstairs? We used to meet for tea and cookies and talk about everything from our husbands to the weather. I made some cranberry puffs for us. I'd love to see it and catch up with each other."

Aggie smiled and her face glowed. "I would love that. Let's go upstairs."

They started toward the stairs when Aggie stopped and turned to the others still standing in the entryway.

"Oh my goodness. I forgot all about you! Why don't you join us?"

"Thank you, Aunt Aggie, but I'm needing to find a few older records for a case I'm working on. I've asked Lainey and Francy to help me. You go ahead. We won't be long."

She nodded and started back up the stairs. "Vera, I can't tell you how often I…"

They watched as the two old friends disappeared upstairs. They quickly headed to the kitchen and down the stairs to the basement. Francy put down the large purse she was carrying and dumped the contents on the floor.

"A shovel, flashlights, and…" he paused to take a second glance. "Tell me that is not one of our old police laundry bags."

Francy grinned. "They were going to throw these away when they bought new ones. They make great clothes storage bags."

It was Sarge who rolled his eyes this time. He picked up the shovel and looked at Lainey.

"I suppose I'm the muscle now?"

She ignored his comment but winked at him. "I tried the door, but it's stuck. Can you get it open?"

They walked across the small room to the metal door. Sarge pushed and pulled and beat on the stubborn door with the shovel until it finally yielded. He stood back and wiped off the drops of sweat that had formed on his forehead.

Lainey picked up a flashlight, shining it into the dark opening. Cobwebs hung between the walls and draped across the ceiling. They shimmered as if they were wet from dew when Lainey's light hit them.

Francy sniffed the air and coughed. "It smells musty like the basement, but there is something else here. It reminds me of the formaldehyde we used in biology class for our bug collections. It makes me want to gag."

They had only walked a few feet when Sarge stopped them. The stairway going up to the old parking garage stood in front of them.

"Lainey, hand me the flashlight."

He took it and carefully began looking between the wooden steps. Several had been broken or had rotted over time. Suddenly, he handed the light back to Lainey.

"Hold this over here. I think I see something."

Lainey grabbed the light and leaned closer to Sarge. He bent down, pulled pieces away from two steps, and threw them aside. Francy was straining to see what was hidden, but Sarge's body was in her line of sight.

Sarge got up and dusted his pant legs off. He looked at Lainey and grinned widely. "It's here."

Lainey clapped her hands and looked at Sarge. "It had to be here… It had to be!"

"What had to be here? What is it?" Francy tried to move Sarge out of the way to look behind the steps, but he stopped her.

"I'm sorry, but you're going to have to wait." He turned her around and gave her a little nudge back toward the door. "We're leaving. Lainey, after you."

Francy complained and grumbled as they walked through the basement and back to the main floor. She was still mad when she went upstairs to tell her mom it was time to leave.

"I had the nicest chat with Aggie," Vera said as they walked out to their cars. Before opening her car door, she turned to face Sarge and smiled. "What did you steal?"

He laughed. "Vera, you're amazing. Thank you for being you." He hugged her and got in the front seat of Francy's car.

"Francy?"

"I have not a clue, Mom," Francy said disgustedly. "I'm only the driver."

Vera looked at Lainey and shrugged her shoulders. "What's wrong with her?"

"Sarge was teasing her about the numerous speeding tickets she had gotten. Thanks for helping us."

She waved to her, not wanting to engage in any more conversation, and got in the backseat of Francy's car. The three sat silently for several minutes before Francy fastened her seatbelt and looked at Sarge.

"Care to tell your hired help where to take you?"

"You mean tell you where to go?" Sarge asked. "I've wanted to do that a few times over the years." He looked back at Lainey and they both started laughing.

"Funny, you're *really* funny."

CHAPTER 16

Mirror Falls was the topic of every news broadcast across the state for the next several days. The same reporters and crews that had swarmed the town only two weeks prior, were back shoving their microphones in the faces of anyone who would speak to them. They interviewed people in front of the Backwater Restaurant, at the Dip and Chip convenience stores, in front of the Catholic church, and Babe's House of Caffeine.

Francy had heard nothing from Lainey since that morning at the museum. Vera, trying to cheer her up, invited her over for dinner.

"That was the best meatloaf I've had in a long time. Thanks, Mom," Francy said.

"I know it's one of your favorites."

They were watching KWBB, Vera's favorite news station while cleaning up the kitchen. They both stopped what they were doing when Dave Olivier, one of their reporters, came on camera.

"I have with me one of the most prominent citizens of Mirror Falls, Marvin Jackson. He has agreed to talk exclusively with KWBB about the ongoing murder investigation of Quincy Yelnick."

The camera panned out to show Marvin standing beside the reporter. They were in front of the Mayor's office at city hall.

"Mr. Jackson, is it true that you were partners with Quincy Yelnick?"

"Yes. We were partners in the Dip and Chip convenience stores. I'm devastated over this tragic loss."

"I understand that you came forward as a key witness to a violent altercation between Yelnick and the man currently in police custody, Shep Morton. Tell us what you saw."

Marvin looked directly into the camera, moving over slightly to make sure his face was centered in the frame. "I had taken a few friends to the Backwater that night and while we were eating, we heard two men arguing loudly. Our table was facing the kitchen door and I was shocked when I saw my partner running through the restaurant toward the front entrance."

"Why was he running?"

"Morton was chasing him and threatening him. The man is known for having a brutal temper, but I've never seen him in one of his angry outbursts. Before I knew what was happening, he had thrown Quincy into the wall and was yelling that he would kill him. Quincy got up and ran out the front door."

"That must have been difficult to witness. What happened then?"

"We were all stunned. Morton didn't say anything to anyone. He stormed back through the restaurant and into the kitchen. The next morning when I heard Quincy had been murdered, I felt it my duty to call the police and tell them what I saw."

"That was a brave thing to do. If more people would do the same, Mirror Falls would be a much better town."

Francy pointed the remote toward the television and changed the channel. "I'm sick and tired of hearing this." She threw the remote on the couch in frustration.

"Have you heard from Lainey or Sarge?" Vera asked.

"No. I've left messages for her, but she hasn't responded."

"I visited Shep again yesterday. My heart goes out to him. Why can't they let him out on bail? Why does he have to sit in that horrible cell?" Her bottom lip quivered and her voice cracked. She didn't hide the tears that rolled down her cheeks.

"Mom, we know Shep is innocent. And we know Lainey and Sarge must have reasons for being so distant. They're doing their best to help him. We have to trust them."

Vera nodded. "I know. I hear people saying terrible things about Shep and my heart aches not only for him, but for poor Sally. How many times did our nice little town laugh and ridicule him? I realize now what Sally must have felt during those times. She never stopped believing in him. She was an exceptionally strong woman."

"You are, too, Mom. Shep's name is going to be cleared."

The doorbell rang several times, startling the two. Vera dried her eyes while Francy got up to see who it was.

"Who in the world could that be?" Vera said aloud. She stood up and saw Lainey walking in the room.

"I should be mad at you, but I'm so glad to see you!" she ran to give her a hug. "Tell me you have found a way to save Shep."

Lainey smiled. "You two got a minute? I have something I want to ask you."

They walked over to the kitchen table and sat down. Francy, still a bit upset that she hadn't been included the past few days, tried to be angry with her friend. But, she couldn't.

"What do you need? Mom and I will do whatever you ask."

"Vera, would you be willing to dress up in your cat burglar outfit again? You know, like you did a few years ago when I tried to sneak evidence out of Sarge's office?"

"Only if I can wear my gloves and stocking cap."

"That's perfect," she replied. "Francy, how many of those police dirty clothes bags do you have?"

"Three, I think. Why?"

"Would you mind if I sewed them together, so it makes one, long bag?"

Francy looked puzzled for a moment. Then a huge grin splashed across her face.

"A body bag, right?"

Lainey nodded. "Can I take them with me tonight?"

"Sure," Francy answered. "They're in the front closet."

"I need you both to meet me in the morning at the old museum parking garage at 6 a.m. I'll explain when you get there. I'm sorry I can't share more details, but I'm trying to protect both of you."

Francy looked at Vera. "Do you want Mom to bring the clothes with her?"

"No. It's important that she's wearing them when she walks into the garage." Lainey pulled a small package out of her backpack and handed it to Vera.

"You'll need these."

Vera turned the package over and over in her hand. She looked at Lainey.

"What's this?"

"Open it, Mom. I want to see what it is."

She carefully took the lid off the package and took out a black plastic egg.

"What in the world do you want me to do with this?"

"Tomorrow, it's very important that you are wearing what's inside that egg."

Vera twisted the top off the egg and pulled out a black pair of gloves.

"Thank you, but I already have a black pair of gloves. They're leather, remember?"

Lainey laughed. "These are special. Try them on."

Francy watched as her mom carefully put on the gloves, then looked at Lainey in surprise.

"Skeleton gloves?" Vera asked. "The tops are painted white like skeleton hands."

"Remember, it's very important that you are wearing these when you walk into the garage."

"If you say so. But they won't make my hands look any younger!"

"Please ride together and park over by Jeff's Cleaners. It's only a couple of blocks away. You'll see either my car or Sarge's cruiser parked in that block, too."

"I'll drive," Francy answered. "Where do we meet you?"

"Walk over to the front entrance of the garage. On the right hand side of the double garage door is a steel door. It has a *building condemned, do not enter* sticker on it. Knock on the door and I'll open it."

"You got it. How long will we be there?"

"A couple of hours or so I hope." Lainey stood up and picked up her backpack.

"You can't stay any longer?" Vera asked. "I wanted to play a hand or two of cards."

Lainey shook her head. "I've got a ton to do. Thank you both for doing this. Everything will be clear tomorrow, I promise."

She took the three clothes bags out of the closet, said goodbye, and drove over to the police station where Sarge was waiting for her in the rear parking lot.

"Ready for a long night, Maynard?"

"Yes, sir. Vera and Francy are on board. What about the film crew?"

"Looks like things are in place. Let's get some coffee on the way."

"I'm always ready for a skinny mocha frappe."

They walked over to his patrol car and both got inside. He started the car and his computer lit up instantly.

Sarge adjusted a few buttons and then looked at Lainey. "I've asked this before, but are you 100% sure?"

"I'd bet my life on it," she answered. "I trust Snoops…and you."

"Buckle up, then. This could turn out to be one heck of a ride."

The next day, Melvin and Marvin Jackson arrived at the law office of Schilling, Tate, and Anderson promptly at 1 p.m. They had both received letters that morning from their attorney, Jack Tate, urgently requesting they meet regarding Marvin's partnership in the Dip and Chip Convenience stores.

Marvin had called his dad as soon as the courier delivered the letter.

"A letter from Tate was just del…"

"I know. I got the same letter." Melvin Jackson interrupted.

"It's about time he contacted me about taking full owner-ship of the stores."

He could hear his dad breathing over the phone, but he didn't respond immediately.

"Dad? Did you hear me?"

"Yes, yes, I heard you."

"Let's get the paperwork signed and get those stupid stores on the market. They've been nothing but a drain on my inheritance!"

"You listen to me," Melvin's voice was sharp and harsh. "There is something wrong here. Why didn't Tate pick up the phone and call us like he usually does? And why the urgency?"

Marvin had heard that tone in his Dad's voice only a few times. His heart began to race and he panicked.

"Dad, I can't be blamed for anything! I did what you asked, just like before."

"Stop panicking, you idiot. I need to think."

Marvin had shown up at his Dad's house around noon. As soon as Melvin saw his son, his temper flared.

"You're drunk again. I didn't think you could be more of a disappointment to me, but I was wrong."

"I was scared. I only had a few drinks to calm my nerves."

"Don't waste your lame excuses on me. Get into the kitchen. I'll sober you up if I have to poor a pot of hot coffee down your throat."

Now, the two sat in silence in front of the law office. Melvin had driven and he threatened his son once more before they went inside.

"You're going to keep your mouth shut and only speak if I tell you to. Got it?"

Marvin nodded. His head was pounding and he felt jittery from all the coffee he had consumed.

They got out of the car and walked inside the office. The receptionist greeted them.

"Good afternoon. I'll let Mr. Tate know you are here."

She pushed a button on the desk phone and said, "The Jacksons are here to see you."

"Send them to the main conference room. I'm waiting for them."

The two men nodded and walked down the familiar hallway to the conference room. The door was closed.

Melvin didn't bother to knock. He opened the door and Marvin followed him inside.

"Tate, what's this all about?" Melvin demanded. "What's so important that..." his voice trailed off when he realized there were two other people standing at the back of the room.

Jack Tate was standing at one end of the long conference table.

"Please, Mel. You both need to sit down."

Marvin started walking toward a chair, but his Dad stopped him.

"Not until you tell me what this is about. And why are they here?" Melvin crossed his arms as an act of defiance.

Sarge and Lainey said nothing. Their faces gave no indication of emotion as they looked at Jack.

"This is regarding Quincy's will. He requested law enforcement be at the meeting as well."

Melvin smirked. "Then what is she doing here? She's not an officer."

"She has been working with me on the investigation into Yelnick's death. I felt her information could prove vital to finding his murderer," Sarge said flatly.

Melvin glared at him, then turned his fiery gaze back to Jack Tate.

"You're my attorney. Isn't this a conflict of interest?"

"Please, Mel. Sit down," Jack said forcefully.

Melvin uncrossed his arms and sat down on the left side of the table. He motioned for Marvin to sit next to him.

Sarge and Lainey sat down directly across the table from the two men. They avoided looking across the table and kept their eyes on Tate.

Jack had walked over to the wall directly in front of the table, taking a remote from it's pocket that was attached to wall. He hit a button and a large flat screen descended from the ceiling.

"Get on with it, Tate. I don't need any of your fancy investment charts or slides."

Jack kept the remote in his hand and walked over to stand next to Marvin's chair.

"Very well. As you know, I am the executor of Quincy Yelnick's will. As such, it is my duty to inform you of his last wishes. He requested this video be shown in the event of his death."

CHAPTER 17

Melvin wasn't looking at the screen. He was staring into Lainey's face.

She returned his gaze with an icy stare.

You're not intimidating me, mister.

"Please, watch the screen," Tate said as he hit the button and dimmed the lights in the room.

The white screen turned into a picture of Melvin and Quincy standing in front of a large truck. They were smiling and pointing to the banner stenciled on the driver's cab door. J. Y. Transports.

Melvin didn't move and the picture stayed up for several minutes.

"Yes, we started that company. Can't you fast forward this? I've got important mayoral duties to attend to."

The screen faded and when the next scene appeared, Marvin groaned and put his head down on the table. His dad didn't seem to notice.

The photo of Melvin and Marvin at the Hill Annex Mine appeared. Yelnick was standing in the background.

Tate stopped the video. "I must tell you that the following photos could be disturbing."

Sarge pulled his gaze away from Tate and stared intently at Melvin Jackson. Lainey noticed the tension in his jaw and quietly touched the side of his arm with her hand. He looked at her and she winked. He took a breath and tried to relax.

Melvin grunted. "Enough theatrics, Tate. You're not presenting closing arguments in front of a jury, you know."

"Very well." He hit the play button and the mine picture dissolved into a black and white photo taken at a short distance away from its subject. It was a boat, ready to be launched onto a lake. A person was loading something into it.

The room became deathly quiet. Melvin's expression hardened and his face turned red.

Marvin raised his head and the frightened look in his eyes gave proof that he was about to cry.

Sarge leaned forward in his chair and spoke directly to the older Jackson. "That appears to be you in the photo. And if I'm not mistaken, that boat was owned by your parents."

Melvin slammed his fist down onto the table. The loud sound made Lainey jerk.

"That's Larry, you incompetent fool!"

Sarge didn't flinch. "What's Larry doing? Looks like he's putting something into the boat."

The screen suddenly zoomed in clearly revealing that a young man was indeed putting something into the boat. A lifeless body.

Marvin's mouth was open and the confused look on his face said he was seeing this for the first time.

"Uncle Larry killed someone?" he sputtered loudly. "Why didn't you tell me?"

Melvin said nothing and looked straight ahead.

Jack clicked the remote once again. A newspaper article appeared with the headline circled.

The video slowly zoomed in on the words *Jackson boy injured while trying to save family's barn.*

Lainey saw Melvin's face change for the second time since the meeting began. When he saw the headlines, the fury in his eyes was replaced by fear. He blinked several times, bit his lip, and looked down at his hands.

Tate looked at Melvin, then at Sarge. "Should I go on?"

Sarge nodded.

A photo of large metal barrels neatly stacked in what looked like a cave appeared. They were rusty and the painted labels on them were faded. But their message was clear.

Danger. Liquid Pesticides.

The pictures on the screen began changing more quickly, creating a collage of photos. Page after page of journal entries showing payments from Jackson to Yelnick flashed across the screen. Scenes of parties on the *Ultimo Ganador* showed Quincy and Marvin dancing and drinking with various women in scanty swimsuits.

Marvin stood up slowly. "Dad..."

"Sit down," Melvin instructed his son. "Shut up and sit down."

When a bank security deposit box appeared on the screen, Sarge stood up and walked to the back of the room. Lainey stayed focused on the men sitting opposite her.

As that photo dissolved into the next one, Tate paused the video, turned up the lights, and looked at Melvin.

"This is where I am to read you the following letter," Tate said as he walked to sit down at the head of the table. Behind him, the picture of an open security box seemed to engulf the entire room.

Tate took a letter from his pocket, unfolded it, and began to read.

Well, Tate, old buddy. If you're reading this, I guess our illus-trious Mayor has finally succeeded in getting rid of me. He always did think he was smarter than anyone else. Melvin, I bet you're sitting down hearing this and trying hard to lie your way out of this predicament, too. Oh, you've become a great liar over the years. There's probably none better, I'll give you that.

Since I can't milk you for money anymore, I thought I'd get the last word in. I may be dead, but you're going on a trip worse than death. The news will have a field day. You and your dumb kid will lose everything, even that precious boat of yours. You thought I was ignorant, didn't you? Well, you're about to see what a genius I was.

The police should be listening to this, too. Maybe they are sitting next to you? I would have enjoyed seeing you squirm! Don't worry. By the time you hear this, the police will already have found the evidence I left behind for them.

Well...I guess that's all I have to say. I feel almost sad that I can't watch you suffer any longer. Someday you'll have to admit...I got the last laugh. So long, Larry. And good riddance. You're getting what you deserve.

The silence in the room was deafening. Jack put the letter back in his pocket, took the remote once more and resumed the video. He looked over at Melvin.

The man looked as if a bucket of ice water had been thrown in his face. His eyes were glued to the image that now appeared on the screen.

It was a young Quincy Yelnick standing in front of the remains of a burned building. He was holding a gas canister in one hand and giving a 'thumbs up' sign with the other. Several more gas cans were on the ground in front of his feet.

Quickly the picture faded into a dark room. The camera zoomed in on a large bag lying on a dirt floor. The camera was moving closer to the bag when it turned quickly to the right and zoomed out.

From a distance, two blurry forms were approaching the bag. As they slowly got closer to the camera, the images came into focus. The room was dark, but it was apparent that the two objects were a pair of hands. They looked strange, almost iridescent. Just as the focus became crystal clear, a skeleton's hand pointed a bony finger toward the bag. Then the screen went black. The video ended.

Marvin jumped up and tried to run from the room. When he opened the door, police officers restrained him and brought him back inside.

"I'm not taking the blame for this! Daddy, you need to fix this!" He cried out.

Melvin didn't move.

Lainey watched as the man sitting across from her shrank into his seat. His shoulders fell and he slumped down into the chair. She almost felt sorry for him until she remembered how evil he was.

Sarge walked over to him, took hold of his arm, and brought him to his feet. "Mr. Mayor, I'm arresting you on suspicion of murder. You have the right to remain silent..."

It took several weeks for the news frenzy over the Jackson case to ease up. Shep and Vera had invited their friends to dinner at the Backwater on the Fourth of July. They were waiting on the porch to welcome Francy, Lainey, and Sarge as they arrived.

"Sarge, I'm so glad you could make it." Shep put out his hand.

"Thank you for the invitation, but this wasn't necessary," he said, shaking hands.

"We wanted to thank you and this is the only way we know how," Vera replied. "He's been cooking all day."

"Wow, it smells delicious," Francy said. "I've been hungry since Shep invited us for dinner."

She gave them both a big hug.

Lainey waited until Francy had gone inside before speaking to the couple.

"Shep you look great! It's been a crazy few weeks, hasn't it?"

He smiled. "It has at that." He hugged her and she noticed a little tear in the corner of his eyes.

"You believed me. You believed in the dreams. How can I ever thank you?"

"No thanks are necessary. Just keep Vera safe and out of trouble, okay?"

He grinned and Vera playfully punched his shoulder.

"Hey! I never cause trouble!" she laughed.

As Lainey walked inside, she noticed only one table sitting in the middle of the room. Sarge and Francy were standing beside the table. They looked puzzled too.

"What's up with this? Where's your other tables?" Sarge asked.

"You are my special guests this evening. The entire restaurant is at your service. Please, sit down. Vera and I will bring your dinner."

They walked to the kitchen as each person took a chair. A scarlet red cloth covered the table with four drippy wax candles placed in a square in the center. They resembled little soldiers assigned to protect what was sitting between them.

The three friends gazed at the unique centerpiece and then began laughing.

"Only Mom and Shep could have come up with this idea!"

Sarge smiled as he picked up the piece. "It's the small end of a fishing pole. Looks like the line goes down into that bucket."

A little note on the pole instructed *Reel her in!* Sarge cranked the makeshift reel a couple of times. The little rod bent down as a black skeleton glove appeared above the bucket.

"She'll never let you live this down, Lainey. She thinks she's a first class cat burglar now!" Francy chuckled.

Shep and Vera had prepared a feast of the groups favorite foods. There was fresh baked garlic bread and spaghetti with meatballs for Francy. Sarge enjoyed a deep dish shepherd's pie with green beans and a big glass of red beer.

"You two have outdone yourselves," Lainey managed to say between bites of homemade chicken enchiladas. "This cornbread is to die for!"

After they had eaten as much as they possibly could, Vera brought a huge pot of coffee from the kitchen. Shep followed her with a three layer red velvet cake.

As they relaxed over coffee and dessert, the conversation turned to the upcoming Jackson trial.

"I'm still unclear on how you figured out Melvin was actually Larry." Shep told Sarge. "They were identical twins."

"Lainey is the one who first had the idea," he replied and raised his coffee cup to her.

"I can't take all the credit," she smiled. "Marvin is the one who first made me suspect something was going on. When he confronted me the morning the boat was recovered, I remembered Shep's dream. I just knew there was more to the story."

"The guys at the department said Marvin cried like a baby and spilled everything he knew," Francy said. "They couldn't shut him up! Some football hero he turned out to be."

"What really happened all those years ago? It's hard to believe Melvin would pay Yelnick money for more than forty years."

"Blackmail is a powerful weapon," Sarge said. "We think Yelnick watched Larry kill his brother and put him in the boat. When he confronted Jackson, they came up with a plan to keep Larry's secret."

"Larry has admitted that he had Yelnick set fire to the barn. And he purposely went inside to burn his hands. He figured if the body were ever found, there would be no way he could be fingerprinted," Francy said.

"What he didn't know was that Yelnick kept copies of everything to guarantee his stream of money continued," Sarge added.

"Those were the pictures I didn't share with you. It was in the papers we took from the museum," Lainey said. "Sorry, but I knew it was one of the Jackson twins. And since our Mayor…"

"*Former* Mayor," Vera corrected.

"Our *former* Mayor was a powerful man and I knew he had to be involved, I didn't want you to be in danger."

"So Yelnick took the picture and used it to blackmail Melvin…I mean Larry…all these years?" Shep asked.

Sarge shook his head. "Yes, he did. There was more evidence of his involvement in his security deposit box."

"How did you find out about the security box?" Vera asked.

"Yelnick's will directed Tate to open the security box at the bank with a law enforcement official present. Fortunately, Jack did just that. Once he saw the journal entries, the picture of the boat and the photo of Quincy holding a gas can, he did everything he could to help us."

"Why didn't you arrest Jackson then? Shep could have been released from jail days earlier." Vera questioned.

"The evidence in the box could have sealed Jackson's fate. But I needed a way to confront him. Catch him off guard. That's when Lainey told me her idea of making a video."

"It's so hard to believe he's been living a lie for more than forty years!" Shep exclaimed.

Francy ate her last bite of cake and took a sip of coffee. "The barrels of pesticides were underneath the stairs in the old garage entry. Why didn't you want me to see them?"

Lainey and Sarge exchanged glances, then smiled at each other.

"Seems Maynard has a guardian angel named Snoops."

"Yes, I do! I asked Snoops to do research on the trucking company partnership. Looks like Yelnick had been illegally selling liquid pesticides in Canada without Jackson's knowledge."

"When Quincy was arrested for the parking violations, he was afraid Jackson would find out and his source of black-mail money would dry up," Sarge continued.

"Why is the picture taken at the mine significant? Everyone knew they were partners." Francy asked.

"Good question. The reason I didn't want you to look under the stairs that morning wasn't to hide the barrels from you. It was to hide the bags of mine tailings on top of them."

"Mine tailings?"

"Waste ore from the mining process. Every mine must get rid of the waste so they create what's called a tailing pile. Hill Annex was no exception. And Quincy was smart enough to mention those in his little security box as well."

Francy shrugged her shoulders. "How in the world are mine tailings and barrels of pesticides connected?"

"Yelnick was particularly good at protecting himself. He made lots of notes over the years. Each time there was evidence against Jackson, he would make a copy of it. One copy he mailed or gave to Jackson and the original he put in the box along with the note."

"The last dated note we found was written a few days after Quincy's arrest for the parking tickets. It said that he had been secretly dumping excess barrels of pesticide he couldn't sell to Canada into the tailings pile at the mine," Sarge explained.

"Once Jackson decided to pull out of the trucking company, Yelnick mailed him the picture taken at the mine and threatened to expose him as the master mind of the illegal pesticide deals," Lainey said.

"We tested the tailings found in the basement. They tested positive for Glyphosate," Sarge said.

"Then how did the barrels and those photos get into the basement of the museum?" Shep asked.

"Quincy helped when the old records were first put in the basement for storage. Years later, when he learned that entry was condemned, he must have slipped into the basement before it was sealed and hid the barrels and piling bags for safe keeping."

They sat quietly for a few moments. Each one lost in their own thoughts. Vera was the first one to speak.

"I've never starred in a video before. I have to tell you that I'm a bit disappointed in the editing."

Francy looked at her mom. "What are you talking about? What editing?"

"For more than two hours, I walked back and forth through the garage. I must have pointed at that darn bag of bricks fifty times. And what thanks did I get for my efforts? My hands wearing ugly skeleton gloves were the only part of me seen!"

The group laughed.

"But it was the most important part of the entire video, Mom," Francy chuckled.

"Did anyone ever tell Jackson that you and Sarge made the video?" Shep asked.

"No. Every piece of evidence in the video, including the letter from Quincy, was found inside the security box," Lainey replied.

Francy looked from Sarge to Lainey and back to Sarge. "Wait. Mom's hands and my laundry bags weren't in his security box."

Sarge grinned. "Did you know that Marvin is extremely scared of ghosts? If watching the video didn't make Melvin, aka Larry, confess, we needed a backup plan. Vera, your bony skeleton hands were perfect."

"Is that right? In that case, I guess I can forgive you for editing me out."

Shep gave her a hug. "She's amazing, isn't she?"

"Now don't get all sappy on me," Vera teased. "My daughter can hear you!"

Sarge pushed back his chair and rubbed his belly. "Shep, that was delicious. I've got to be going. Thanks so much."

"Yes, thank you both," Francy and Lainey said at the same time.

"We'll do this again soon," Shep replied.

He and Vera waved to each of them as they got in their respective cars and drove off.

CHAPTER 18

L ainey slept well for the first time in weeks. She woke up early and wondered what the day would bring. She didn't have to wait long to find out.

Her cell phone rang when she stepped out of the shower. She noticed it was Francy and figured she could return her call after she dressed.

A couple minutes later, Francy called again.

Something's up if she's calling again.

"Hello? Francy?"

"Are you sitting down?"

"No. Should I be?"

"Mom and Shep have made the front page of the morning newspaper."

Lainey hesitated. She didn't know whether to laugh or ask what had happened.

"They are both sitting in the backseat of my car. Sarge told them they needed to tell you in person."

"Sarge? Tell me what?"

"I'll be at your house in a few minutes. That's all I can say."

Lainey ended the call and walked slowly from her bedroom to the front door. She opened it and stepped onto the porch to wait for them.

What in the world have they done? Surely Shep hasn't gotten involved in the Jackson case again?

She watched as a car pulled into her driveway. Francy got out and slammed her door. She stomped toward the porch, not looking back to see if her passengers had gotten out of the car.

"You will *not* believe this!" she said to Lainey, waving the newspaper she was carrying in the air.

"What? What's happened?"

Francy stepped on the porch and stood next to Lainey. She was fuming.

"Calm down. I can see steam shooting out your ears. What's happened?"

"Oh no…you ask them what's happened. I'm going inside and get a big bottle of water from your fridge." Francy turned and walked inside the house.

Lainey watched as Vera and Shep got out of the car and came up to the porch.

"What's going on? You're on the front page of the newspaper?"

They looked at each…and grinned.

"We might be. And if we were, it would have been worth every minute of it!" Shep replied happily.

For once, Lainey didn't have a response.

"Come on inside," Vera said as she took Lainey by the hand. "You'll be fine and Francy will be fine. He couldn't prove a thing."

Shep opened the door for them and the three walked inside. Francy was sitting at the table with a bottle of water in one hand and the newspaper in the other.

Shep pulled out a chair for Lainey and one for Vera and stood behind her chair.

"Would one of you *please tell me what's going on*? Why are you in the newspaper? And how is Sarge involved?" Lainey blurted out.

"I had to make another trip to the police station this morning. Seems bait-shop-Charlie filed a complaint." Francy replied.

"Charlie Crowfoot? What kind of complaint?"

Francy pointed her finger at her mother. "You tell her."

Shep put his hands on Vera's shoulders and smiled. "Indecent exposure."

Lainey's mouth dropped open and she looked at him in disbelief.

"Say that again?"

"You heard correctly. Indecent exposure. We used to do it all the time back in my high school days," Shep laughed.

Francy shoved the newspaper over to Lainey. "Take a look at the lower right hand corner of the page."

She picked up the paper and a grin spread across her face. The photo was dark and obviously taken in the middle of the night. But it very clearly showed two people's naked derrieres sticking out the windows on the driver's side of a car.

"They *mooned* Charlie?" She burst out laughing. Shep and Vera did too.

Lainey gave the paper back to Francy.

"How did this get to the newspaper? And why did Sarge tell you to bring them here?"

Francy finished the bottle of water before answering.

"It appears a car drove up to Charlie's house and someone began honking its horn loudly. The noise woke him up and he looked out the window. What he saw made him mad. He grabbed his cell phone and snapped this photo."

Vera and Shep kept smiling but remained silent.

"Charlie got in his car, went down to the station, and filed a complaint against them for indecent exposure."

Vera rolled her eyes. "He looked so ridiculous in those pajamas covered with little swimming fishes. And besides that, the man has never seen my backside!"

Lainey closed her eyes and tried to bite her lip to keep from laughing.

"Anyway," Francy continued, "because he named Mom and Shep, they were brought down to the station for questioning."

"What was Sarge going to do? I told him it wasn't us and it wasn't either of our cars," Shep said innocently. "I offered to let him compare my backside to one in the picture, but for some reason, he declined."

Lainey couldn't hold back any longer. She burst out laughing and couldn't stop. Every time she looked at Vera or Shep, she started to laugh again.

"Oh my word," she said. "I need to catch my breath."

A smile slowly appeared on Francy's face.

"Did you really ask Sarge to look at your backside?" she asked Shep.

He nodded. "Your Mom did too."

That comment made the laughter start once more. This time Francy joined in.

After they had gathered their composure, Lainey picked up the paper once more.

"So how *did* the newspaper get this picture?"

Francy pointed again to Vera and Shep. "Charlie claims someone took his phone while he was giving his statement and emailed it to them. You two wouldn't happen to know anything about that, would you?"

They both shrugged their shoulders.

Vera grinned and said, "Why, Francine Baines, you know I'm not a thief. I'm a cat burglar for heaven's sake."

. . .

WANT TO JOIN LAINEY AND HER FRIENDS ON THEIR NEXT adventure? Read an excerpt from Book 3 following this page! Click the link below to start your adventure now! Free in Kindle Unlimited!

Curtain Call At Brooksey's Playhouse

PREVIEW OF CURTAIN CALL
AT BROOKSEY'S PLAYHOUSE

Present Day

Lainey plopped down in her favorite recliner and flipped on the TV. Her cat, Powie, jumped onto her lap as the first strains of The Late Show with Stephen Colbert began. It had been a long, exhausting day and she was more than ready to unwind.

"I made a lot of headway in the investigation today. Wish my Keurig wasn't on the fritz. I could use a mocha frappe," she said as she stroked the cat's back. Powie purred, squirmed a bit to get comfortable, and immediately began snoring.

"So much for listening to how my day went," she said quietly, looking down at the spoiled cat.

Lainey had been a fraud investigator for years and ten years ago, when her company relocated her from Houston, Texas to the tiny town of Mirror Falls, Minnesota, she wondered how many cases she would actually be given. To her amazement, her workload had become larger, not smaller.

She tried to listen to the monologue from the television program, but her thoughts kept re-visiting her first cases in Mirror Falls. Memories of meeting the Whoopee group and the Sullivans, the Governor's Fishing Openers, and, of course, Sarge, brought smiles and shivers at the same time. She paused for a moment before picking up her cell phone. "Call Francy," she said.

"Girl, what on earth are you doing calling me during the Late Show?" Francy demanded with a chuckle. "Is everything okay?"

"Has it really been ten years since I moved here?" Lainey said softly. A shudder ran down her spine as if someone had poured freezing water down the neck of her shirt.

"Come to think about it, I guess it has been. We've had a few adventures since then, haven't we?" Francy replied.

Lainey grinned. "Remember the Helvig case? That's when I first met you and joined the Whoopee group."

"I haven't thought about old Brooksey in a long time. Her murder rocked Mirror Falls, that's for sure."

"We didn't eat at the China Palace for months after that," Lainey chuckled. "Vera thought it was bad luck."

"I tried to tell her that the new owners had no connections to Ru Fong or Brooksey's Playhouse," Francy replied. "She didn't believe me until the McMurray's moved in next door to her."

"Do you remember when she took her famous coconut bars over to welcome them to the neighborhood? When they told her they were the new owners of the Palace, she got so flustered, she dropped the entire plate of bars!" Lainey's eyes were tearing up from laughing so hard.

"That was too funny!" Francy said. It took them both a minute to compose themselves.

"I was working when the call came in about the explosion. I think every officer on the force was there," Francy sighed. There was a seriousness in her voice.

"Things changed in Mirror Falls after that," Lainey said. "Was it worth the cost?"

YOU CAN MAKE A DIFFERENCE

If you've enjoyed my book, please leave a review!
Murder in the Backwater

Reviews are the most important and powerful ways to spread the word about my books.

I believe there is something more effective and personal than any type of ad.

It's you! Building a relationship with committed and loyal readers is powerful!

An honest review will help bring my books to other readers, something no amount of advertising can accomplish!

I humbly and gratefully ask you to spend a few minutes leaving a review if you enjoyed my book. It can be as short or long as you like.

Thank you and blessings on your day!

Laura Hern

ABOUT THE AUTHOR

Laura Hern writes cozy mysteries and romantic comedy. This is her second book in The Lainey Maynard Mystery series.

Her website is www.laurahern.com.

You can connect with Laura on her author Facebook page, on Twitter, and her website.